ONE LAST SHOT

ONE LAST SHOT

THE STORY OF WARTIME PHOTOGRAPHER GERDA TARO

KIP WILSON

▼ VERSIFY

An Imprint of HarperCollinsPublishers

Versify® is an imprint of HarperCollins Publishers.

Library of Congress Cataloging-in-Publication Data
Names: Wilson, Kip, author.
Title: One last shot / by Kip Wilson.
Description: First edition. | New York : Versify, [2023] | Includes author's note. |
    Includes bibliographical references. | Audience: Ages 13 up. | Audience: Grades
    10–12. | Summary: "Tells the story of Gerda Taro, a headstrong photojournalist
    with a passion for capturing the truth amid political turmoil and the first woman
    photojournalist killed in combat"—Provided by publisher.
Identifiers: LCCN 2022009607 | ISBN 9780063251687 (hardcover)
Subjects: LCSH: Taro, Gerta, 1910–1937—Juvenile fiction. | CYAC: Novels
    in verse. | Taro, Gerta, 1910–1937—Fiction. | Photography—Fiction. |
    Photojournalism—Fiction. | Spain—History—Civil War, 1936–1939—Fiction. |
    LCGFT: Biographical fiction. | Novels in verse.
Classification: LCC PZ7.5.W56 On 2023 | DDC [Fic]—dc23
LC record available at https://lccn.loc.gov/2022009607

Typography by David Curtis
22 23 24 25 26 LBC 5 4 3 2 1

First Edition

Para Bernardo

Si muero,
dejad el balcón abierto.
—Federico García Lorca

COMBAT

THE SPANISH SUN

Searing heat bakes

      the dusty earth
      rusty vehicles
      our thirsty bodies

as most soldiers seek
whatever shade
they can snatch
in these trenches

while others call out for me

                  ¡Gerda! ¡Señorita!

trying to protect
      la pequeña rubia
          (the little blonde)
             me

but in fact the cacophony
of battle energizes
me, galvanizes
me, pushes

me to

get every shot
I can.

NEW CAMERAS

I'm on this battlefield lugging around
a cumbersome camera and tripod

                    to film
              motion pictures

along with the one *he* gave me
for photographs

        the
        Leica

and it might seem
too much to carry two

but I need them both
to have any chance

of capturing moments
like this one.

CLOSE-UP

Bullets fly
artillery booms
officers yell
soldiers charge

and I
      crouch
      shoot
      follow
the action

closer to the line

between
us
and
them

      also known as the line

between

      life
          and
death.

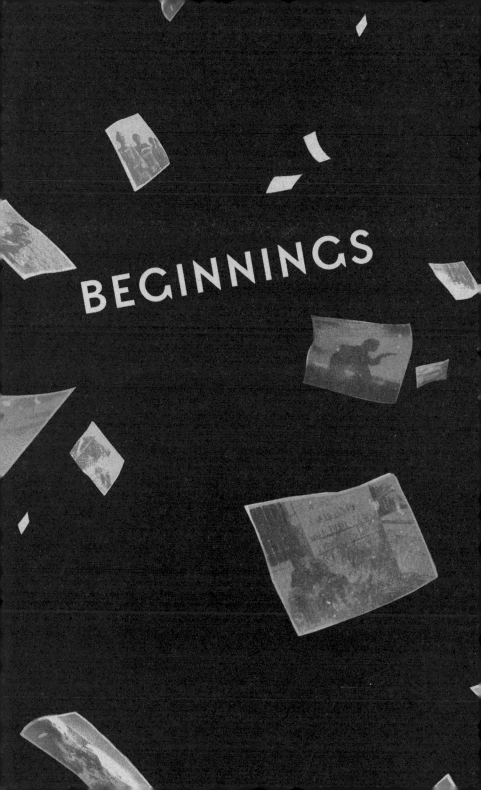

BEGINNINGS

NAMES

My parents have been
      Heinrich
            and
     Gisela
my whole life

yet sometimes they still
     slip up

          calling the other
             Hersch
                 or
            Gittel

which is probably why
they made sure
to give us children
good German names

     Gerda
     Oskar
     Karl

        right from the start.

LIGHTING THE CANDLES

Friday nights
      just before sundown
            we light

candles, sing
      the blessing, share
            homemade challah

all seven of us:

me and my mama and papa
Mama's sister, Tante Terra
her husband, Onkel Moritz
my brothers, Oskar
      two years younger than me
and Karl
      two years younger than him

because family
      is stronger
          together.

FAMILY LIFE

Oskar and Karl tend to
     clump
       together
like dumplings just added
to broth

and though Oskar busies
himself being
the best big brother
he can

I can sense
the breath of relief
when he escapes

      joining me
in my quiet corner
of the flat to read
by my side.

SNAPSHOT

Obvious signs
our country
is at war include

nighttime bombings
      whistle, whistle,
      boom, flash

            growling bellies
            rationed sugar
            no milk.

Perhaps less obvious:

my teacher's
black Trauerbinde
on her arm

together with those
immense, empty eyes
indicating

      she's in mourning.

DISGUISE

Outside our home
appearances are
everything

something my parents
understand
all too well

tasking my wardrobe
to Tante Terra
who makes sure

I'm
impeccably
dressed

sacrificing themselves
to give me
every opportunity

they
never
had.

ASHAMED

The other girls are pleasant
enough to me in school
but the first time I
invite them over to
my family's flat

their disdainful glances at

our simple furnishings
the boxes and papers piled up from
        Papa's delivery business
our candlesticks waiting
                    for Shabbat

tell me there's more
than I'll ever understand
keeping me
        outside
their inner circle

tell me that what I feel is
Anderssein
        (being *other*).

The last thing I want
is to be different
so I decide
my home life should be
                    secret
going forward

decide never
to invite anyone
over

        again.

STUTTGART, GERMANY
OCTOBER 1921
TEA WITH TANTE TERRA

Now that I'm eleven years old
Tante Terra has taken charge
of making sure I know
everything a young girl
should know about the world

        including how

certain Germans point

fat fingers of blame
at us Jews anytime
anything goes wrong

        for instance, as if Germany's defeat
        in the Great War were somehow
            our fault

   but

she assures me
it's possible to both

        remain our true selves
        behind closed doors

   and

        assimilate in German spaces
        outside the home

reminding me
what I already know

        that I must always
        try my best
           to blend in.

UMZUG

Today's the day
hundreds of young girls
from all around Stuttgart

including me
parade to the brand-new
Königin-Charlotte-Realschule

on Zellerstraße
construction
just completed

for our
first day
of school.

We're dressed like young brides
in white dresses
flowers crowning our heads

ready to
begin
        anew.

THE OUTSIDER

Sometimes I fit in fine
at the Königin-Charlotte-Realschule
      as fine as the only Jewish girl in class can

          like when I arrive each day
          hair coiffed, smile bright

      like when I solve equations
          write exacting essays
translate poems into French

but on Saturdays
when I still must attend
school in the mornings
      on Shabbat

I take care to avoid
forbidden tasks like
opening classroom doors
writing with my pencil

but I can't avoid sticking out

when it's time to pay

for lunch

because

touching money
      is forbidden too

and instead I suffer strange looks
when I hand a classmate
my money purse
ask her to extract the right coins

        wondering if there's a way
           to ever
        truly fit in.

HOME AND AWAY

At home
I embrace
      quiet moments
      laughter
          love
knowing
this is who I am

but at school

I
step
away
from that self
      bit by bit

knowing
this is who I must be

if I'm ever to find
my own place
in
the
world.

GROWING UP

LOOKING UP

The years pass

our luck changes
our lives change

when Onkel Moritz takes on
Papa as a permanent employee
in his more established delivery business

              fanciful Papa
          always dreaming of more

and I march into a new
year of school like
I run the place myself

which works

not only because I'm
smart and ambitious and a little bit wily

but also because I'm
attractive and coquettish and petite

weapons
that seem
            to matter
                    more.

Of course

it also helps that
        I wear my otherwise
                        unremarkable
                brown hair
        as short as a boy's
                (compared to everyone else's long locks)
because nothing
                boosts a girl's confidence more
                        than fearlessness.

FRIENDSHIP

I've finally worked my way into
the tight-knit fabric
        of schoolmates

but only when I get to know
Meta Schwarz
this year

a girl as fun and
charming as I aim to be

do I feel like I've made
a true friend.

She knows
        that I'm Jewish
        that I'm *other*
and somehow doesn't care.

Still, I keep
my own home cloaked
behind a curtain of mystery
                even from her

but

we go together to her flat after
school each day, where her
entire family welcomes
me into their fold, adopts
me as one of them, gives
me a second home.

PLUCKED

Meta and I adore
today's film stars

       her favorite, Asta Nielsen
            mine, Greta Garbo

and we decide to do
our brows like theirs

painfully plucking
dozens of tiny hairs

filling penciled brows
in sleek lines

transforming ourselves
into modern-day royalty.

MAY 1926
One day

Meta's Onkel Friedrich visits
with his latest purchase
      a camera!

Of course
I've been photographed

for school and family portraits
before

but this is a smaller
handheld camera

without cumbersome
tripods and drapes and plates.

I'm immediately
drawn to it

asking
his permission

to pick it up
examine it

look through
its viewfinder

and my entire perspective
changes.

SNAPSHOT

Onkel Friedrich gathers
us girls together
tells us

Sit still now

and one second later

click!

we burst into
the giggles we were
holding.

While the others
imagine out loud
what it would be like
to be a fashion model

I shake my head
absolutely certain
the last thing I want to do
is spend my days
posing

for someone else.

Instead I picture the scene
through an imaginary viewfinder
                in my mind
cataloging

every
single
detail.

MEMENTO

The next week when
Onkel Friedrich develops

his film, delivers
the photo to Meta

we both laugh with joy,
Meta gushing

over each of our
faces, our looks.

What captivates
me instead is

our giddy exuberance
trapped in time

the moment
preserved.

Another day

Meta and I pull out
her older sister's box of
costume jewelry

do ourselves up fine
with necklaces and
clip-on earrings

adding a healthy dose of
lipstick to our smiles
powder to our cheeks

push the furniture
to one side of the room
and everything's hotsy-totsy.

Meta sets a new jazz recording
on the gramophone
      the Paul Godwin Tanzorchester

and we dance, dance, dance
swapping the lead each time
she sets the needle on the disk

until
our feet can't foxtrot
anymore.

BREAKAWAY

It's gotten late
and though I rush
to make it home
in time for Shabbat

      the silence
      the darkness

that greet me
once I return and
slip out of my heels
at the door, tiptoe
toward the table

is nothing compared to

Mama's stony gaze
unwilling to meet mine

Tante Terra's
raised eyebrows

even Papa's kind eyes
full of disappointment

all adding up to
make me feel
like I've failed
this family.

SILENT TREATMENT

They don't say
            a word to me.
        (They don't have to.)

Silent guilt
weighs
me
down

        follows me into the next week
            when I'm careful

                    to watch the clock
but I'm soon slipping back
          into bad habits
                    because as much as I want
                              to please my parents
          I realize I want
                    to please myself

                                        more.

REBELLION

Now that I've embraced
my teen years
left the girl I once was
                    behind

for cigarettes
          freedom
                    friendship

it sometimes feels like
Tante Terra's the only one
still in my corner
answering unspoken wishes like

a makeup kit

Elizabeth Arden!
for my sixteenth birthday

and an offer to finance
a year abroad
at a finishing school
in Switzerland
            and

I blurt out
        Jawohl!

knowing I'll miss
my family

but
unable to resist

this opportunity to
                    reinvent
myself.

SNAPSHOT

Before I leave
for Switzerland

I pull Oskar
aside

share my stash
with him

books, magazines,
newspaper articles

      secret not because
      Mama and Papa wouldn't approve
      but because they wouldn't
         understand.

Time slows

    tick
    tock
as I look Oskar in the eye

remind him that
though it's cozy in here

      there's a whole world
         out there

and it's his job now
to make sure he and Karl

fling themselves
into it

find their own place
to belong.

PULLY, SWITZERLAND
SEPTEMBER 1927
FINISHING

Meta has convinced her parents
that she needs to attend

finishing school as well
and upon arrival

at the Villa Florissant
in Chamblandes-Pully

we find the sanctuary
of our dreams.

A private residence dedicated
to preparing

young women for futures
in which we are not only

someone's
        daughter, wife, mother

but also our very own
                selves

and we relish
every moment

in the companionship of
other young ladies

some of whom know
exactly what they want

while I'm content
to enjoy the ride on these

literary
voyages

in the pages of the books we read
the texts we translate.

Even if I don't know
exactly where I'm heading

I already look forward
to finding a way to make

a future
for myself.

NICKNAME

The girls start calling me

Poho

short for my last name
        Pohorylle

and it's so thrilling to slip
into this new name
that I fall in love with
                the idea
of trying on
a new self.

SNAPSHOT

Each day here is another
to file away and remember

     click, whirr

my mind capturing
the morning hours filled
with studies of
      languages
      the arts
      proper etiquette

the afternoons with
sports outdoors
long walks along lac Léman
fresh air
      rain, snow, or shine

these shared times reminding
us every day

that young women deserve
to quench our thirst
for knowledge too.

One day

we play a game
looking each other over

      all twenty of us
      all lovely young ladies

and name who has

    best hair
    best eyes

        best legs
        best figure

and of course
the winners shimmer

    with stereotypical standards:
    blond hair, blue eyes

        long legs, hourglass curves
            (yawn).

I possess none
of those things but

I wouldn't trade
my look for anything

and when someone calls out
    best laugh

I'm pleased to see
all heads turn my way

the winner
unanimous.

ALL THIS AND TALENT TOO

It's become obvious
we all possess
certain talents that make
each of us stand
apart from the rest.

Renée's supervisory skills
will take her to the top
of the household she aims
to lead.

Traute plays the piano
so well it's a wonder
she didn't go to a conservatory.

Others excel at
public speaking
poetry
painting

but I shine above all
as the girl of many tongues

improving not only
my fluency in French
            but also my English
        and even a bit of
        Spanish in the mix

convincing the girls
and maybe myself
that one day I'll be
            talking
my way out of trouble
wherever
I go.

JUNE 1928

FINISHED

After a fabulous year
Meta and I prepare
to return home

my suitcase filled with
        papers
        notebooks
        souvenirs

my heart filled with
                    memories

of fun and friendship
and
of the person I've become
                    Poho.

STUTTGART, GERMANY
HOMECOMING

Back in Stuttgart
a joyful reunion
with the whole family
at the Hauptbahnhof

        Papa's hugs and kisses
        Mama's businesslike nod
        Tante Terra's loving smile
        my brothers' playful tussles

and I realize
that I loved being away
but I adore being home too.

I slip into
Friday Shabbat meals
afternoons at Meta's
breakfasts with the newspaper
scouring the want ads
for jobs

but inside I wish
there were a way to push
my two selves
into separate bubbles

        private (for family)
and
            public (for friends)

and still
remain whole.

SUNDAY HOBBY

One of the skills I
picked up at the villa
      tennis

comes in handy
when Meta invites
me to the court

on Sunday afternoon.

It's filled
      with young men and women
      dressed in white
           so pristine

ironic
because

it's the perfect place
for red lipstick
slow winks
and thoughts that
are anything
but pure.

SNAPSHOT

Meta serves the ball
but instead of keeping
my eye on it
as I should

my gaze meets
the clear blue eyes
of the young man
on the neighboring court

and he's tall
and lean and
his chestnut hair
gleams in the sun

and time freezes
as I snap
his photograph
in my mind.

A HINT OF ROMANCE

It all happens blitzschnell

      the tall, handsome man
          approaches
          (even taller up close)
              smiles
    kisses my hand

and when he asks my name
I'm tempted to say Poho
but I restrain
myself, say

    Gerda Pohorylle

and by the time
he introduces himself as

Hans Bote
but call me Pieter

I feel comfortable sharing
my own nickname and soon
our tennis partners are giggling
calling us

Pieter and Poho

already
      in sync

already
      on our way to
            becoming
        a couple.

TEA WITH TANTE TERRA

My conversation
with Tante Terra about Pieter
calls for two spoonfuls of sugar.

So tell me about your
young man.

Well, he's charming.

She smiles, gestures
for me to continue.

He's well-off. Works as a salesman
for an American company.

American? She wrinkles
her nose.

Oh, he's not American.
He's from Bremen, from
a good bourgeois family.

Jewish?

I press my lips together
shake my head.

Oh, Gerda. I don't think
this man is for you.

But I didn't spend
all these years

learning to fit in

     for nothing.

Pieter

soon learns I love
to dance, laugh, live it up.

He's older than me
ready to treat a lady right

so he knows how to spoil
me perfectly

taking me out to
concerts and dinners

lavishly spending
on steak and champagne

letting me see
what a life at his side

would be
like.

SNAPSHOT

We zoom
out of the city
in Pieter's sweet
little Opel
to go swimming
in Cannstatt

and swimming
with him
is like dancing
with him

synchronized
            almost
        choreographed

until we both
come up for air
gasping
treading water
gazes locked
moving
close
closer
closest

our lips
sealed
in a
slippery
kiss.

EXPANDING CIRCLE

While I'm off
spending time with Pieter

Meta's off as well
getting to know local students
going out with them to exclusive
dance clubs and fraternity parties

       places I'm
       not
       welcome.

Though Meta's still always
there for me

the first time I meet
her students and hear
the filthy slander
as they chorus

pointing at the same line
on the front page
of the antisemitic paper
    Der Stürmer

I realize that not only
might my bubble never
overlap with Meta's again

but mine might be in
      danger
of popping.

SLOWDOWN

With these changes
in my social circle

I spend even more
time with Pieter

but some things don't happen
so blitzschnell at all

like my parents
or Tante Terra

welcoming
the idea

of me
falling
for a
gentile

not even when Pieter shows
us all how serious he is

when he asks
me to marry him

and I'm so excited at
the prospect of

the new experience
that I can't help

but say
     yes.

SEALING THE DEAL

Pieter whoops, lifts
         me up, swings
            me in a circle
                legs flying behind me
        then brings me back
    to earth
with a kiss.

WORK AND PLAY

Engaged!
What a gas!

The next months pass
in a blur of
dates

      dinners
      coffees
      parks

interspersed with my classes

at a local business school
for some practical skills

stenography
typing

because no matter what happens
with Pieter
I'm determined
to support myself

but it turns out
a time bomb's ticking
in our family

exploding

when my parents announce
a new opportunity for Papa
ever the dreamer
that will expand the family business
and send our family of five

to Leipzig

also known as
forever
away.

SNAPSHOT

I open my makeup kit
peer at my face
in the mirror

make
expressions
to match
my emotions
from the past
few weeks

    giddy
going out with Pieter

               disgusted
          with Meta's friends

     disappointed
     she's running around with them

           elated
           to be engaged

unsure
about the future

open
to anything.

GOODBYES

Pieter and I are
somber, reserved
when we share a dutiful
embrace, a kiss, a
promise to write

we're still engaged, after all

but later that day
when I bid Meta
farewell

I burst
to pieces
clinging to this person
who still means the world to me

as she clings right back
promising me
our friendship
will last

forever

though I'm not even sure
she believes the words
        herself.

**LEIPZIG, GERMANY
MAY 1929**

NEW CITY

It takes some time to settle in
but months after leaving home

I'm finally swept up
in a group of like-minded people
in Leipzig.

The city is about the same
size as Stuttgart
but somehow more

        electric

especially when it comes
to politics and identity
things that didn't interest me
much before but

     most decidedly
interest me now

          especially since
          for the first time in my life
          I find myself among
          people like me

                    not the bourgeoisie
                    but intellectuals
                    idealists
                    fellow Jews

opening their doors
enthusiastically
letting
me
in.

HOMESICK

I still miss
Meta and Pieter

and the life I left
          behind

but mostly

I'm too busy

getting out
fitting in

  becoming the best me
      I can be.

THINGS I LEARN

The Weimar Republic
is a democracy

with elections held most recently
last year

with more than a dozen political parties
represented in the Reichstag

with more than a dozen groups of
wildly different voices trying to compromise

with coalitions between groups
who range

    from communists and
    socialists fighting
    for workers' rights

to nazis fighting
to push their antisemitic
xenophobic agenda

to moderates
who fall somewhere
        in
        between
who together hold
most of the power.

I lean more left every day myself
even though Papa's sure that
any additional weight
on either end might tip
the balance to topple
        this democracy.

HEADLINES

Just like in Stuttgart
Oskar and I spend
time together reading

        often newspapers with
        headlines like

MASSIVE MAY RIOTS
IN BERLIN

BLOODY MAY 1 BATTLES

VICTIMS OF THE MAY UNREST
19 DEAD, HUNDREDS WOUNDED

but we're also reading
Erich Maria Remarque's
shocking story about the Great War
Im Westen Nichts Neues
(*All Quiet on the Western Front*)
serialized a few months ago.

Each page we read
immerses us

in the horrors
of war

and the dangers
of nationalism

leaving us
as shell-shocked
as the soldiers
themselves.

LEFT WING

It seems clear our country is
heading in two directions

      far

            to the right

and

      far
to the left

and soon there's no doubt
in my mind that
one of these options
is far more dangerous
to people like us

with the way the right attacks
      trade unions
      the stock market
      not to mention us Jews

so I do my part
join Leipzig's left-wing

youth movement

     get to know
     those in its circle

become more
               vehement
in my beliefs.

NEW FRIENDS

I meet
Georg Kuritzkes

     one of the
     movement's leaders

          who's as charming
          as he is passionate
               for the cause

find a new girlfriend in
Ruth Cerf

     who attends high school
     where they allow me to take classes
     to quench my never-ending thirst

for new knowledge

who bursts into a smile
each time she finds me
            waiting for her outside
            in my heels and lipstick

who seems interested
            in Georg
but who also seems to think
I can get anything I want

            including
            him.

I would step aside
for her if she asked

            especially because, well, Pieter

but I can't help but return
Georg's attention

            when she
            doesn't.

DIFFERENCES

It's only when I go back
to Stuttgart for a visit
and Meta meets me
at the station where we
      squeal and
      kiss and
      hug hello

that I realize
that slipping into the past by
simply trying on jewelry and
painting our lips rose red
doesn't seem possible

and even a perfect date
with Pieter only seems
like playacting
when he doesn't want to
discuss important topics
      like politics

so as much as I love them
      and truly I do

my eyes are slowly focusing

on the fact that
an important era of my life

is coming
      to a close.

PEN PALS

The fact is that
long-distance friendships
and boyfriendships
are harder to
maintain

than I initially thought

      even with visits
      and letters

because
          it's simply
              not
     the same

and soon enough I'm not
           engaged
     anymore.

OCTOBER 1929
HEADLINE

Today's news is splattered
across the top of
every paper:

WALL STREET COLLAPSE

and the news that the
stock market in New York
has crashed

leads to the
world markets
tumbling

leading us to worry
about what will come
next.

IT'S A DATE

In Stuttgart, Pieter took
me to tennis

to dinner

but

in Leipzig, Georg takes
    me to political rallies
    to discussion evenings

where we feed
off each other's passion
for this cause

because as much as we both support
the left
we stand as strongly against
                  the right

especially

    the nazis who aim to blame
        us Jews
    for the economic collapse

and soon my life revolves
around typing up documents
handing out pamphlets

living a life filled
with determination
to fight

against those
trying to tip the scales
toward tyranny.

SNAPSHOT

Sometimes when I'm with Georg
    and his friends
I simply watch, wishing
   I had a way
     to record
  the fervor
bouncing from
   one of them to
     the next to
       the next
a single spark
    creating
  a chain reaction.

FEBRUARY 1930
FAMILY LIFE

When I'm not out taking part
in all sorts of activism

with my new friends

my home life
in our new flat remains
much the same

Friday evening Shabbat meals
pooled finances to keep
the family afloat

Mama's worried glances
Papa's loving gazes
        dreamy head in the clouds

Oskar's firm beliefs
growing firmer with
each new fact he learns

even Karl
a teenager too
catching up with the two of us

we five
a nucleus
in this world.

In particular

Oskar has taken to
      reading the pamphlets
      I bring home

              listening to my rants about
              the dangers of nationalism to
                  people like us

              sneaking out
                  a block behind me

as I head for
another rally
seemingly unaware
      yet wholly aware
that he's
      following
            in my footsteps.

SNAPSHOT

At the next rally
I raise my fist

wholeheartedly agreeing
we must fight for

     equality
     solidarity
     workers' rights
         for all

observing the crowd
through an imaginary viewfinder

     click
     click
     click.

Written on these faces
I see
what we aim
     to accomplish

and what we aim
     to abolish
before they take root

         nazism and
         nationalism and
         fascism

a trio ready to rot
this country
to its core.

ANDERSSEIN

When I was a child
the last thing I wanted
was to be *other*

but I really didn't know
how rewarding
it would be

to find my people
my purpose
my place

to become part of something
so much more powerful
than little me.

ELECTION AFTER ELECTION

It's 1930 and
campaign posters paper

the city

as we barrel toward
yet another election
because our country
can't quite seem to figure out
where it's headed.

I hold out hope for the Nazis to lose
their twelve Reichstag seats

    but

their party has been
gaining strength
gaining followers
       looking for someone to blame
       for Germany's problems
and while the rest of the parties

hold far more seats
          together

apart

          we are

                    nothing.

OMINOUS

The results of the
Reichstag elections
are clear from the headline

    VICTORY FOR RADICALISM

    NATIONAL SOCIALISTS NINE TIMES STRONGER
    COMMUNISTS INCREASE
    WEAKENING OF THE CENTER

and while I'm glad to see
the left has at least
made gains

Papa has me worried
about the sagging center
because

the Nazis now boast
the second-strongest party
in the Reich

and we can only bow our heads
and pray their gains
are temporary.

CHANGE

LEIPZIG, GERMANY
JANUARY 1933

HEADLINE

Three
years
later

after
more elections
more clashes between left and right
more antisemitic scapegoating

an ailing, flailing government
        flounders
swearing in the new cabinet
with an impossible
concession.

      PRESIDENT HINDENBURG APPOINTS
      THE LEADER OF THE NATIONAL SOCIALIST PARTY
          ADOLF HITLER
      AS CHANCELLOR

Now that the beating heart
of this country
has been presented
as a precious gift

it's going to be
next to impossible
        to get it back.

STRATEGY

Now that the nazis sit
        in the Reich Chancellery
                we no longer focus
        on beating them
but
        on ways to

                resist.

THRILL RIDE

I help out some
friends with the printing
and copying and distribution
of new leaflets around the city
denouncing what's now
the ruling party and

our words feel more

dangerous

our actions more
important

and I know I should be
        worried
        scared
careful

but besides being
        invested
in this cause

I also realize
I'm ready
for a thrill.

HEADLINE

The morning's paper
blares out the news
no one wanted
to hear:

THE REICHSTAG AFLAME

MULTIPLE FIRES SET

DUTCH COMMUNIST ARRESTED

and it's already clear
the nazis will point fingers
to appear blameless so they
can now take even more

which leads to
torch-bearing bullies
taking to the streets
in celebration

crushing my heart
with waves of
            disappointment
                    disgust
                    despair.

FAMILY LIFE

My parents know
my political beliefs

but they are much more
cautious
            especially Papa

so I'm also

cautious
       to keep them uninvolved

to keep my more radical
                activities
                secret

to keep Oskar safe
as he joins me
and this movement
of rebellion.

DANGEROUS

I let Oskar come along
with me

to slather
walls and columns

with glue, slap
on anti-nazi posters

       one at a time

each one a drop
in the river

drops in the river
we're certain will

add up to
a torrent.

MY BROTHERS

Oskar soon takes Karl
under his wing

    the two of them
    becoming

more like me
every day

    making radical friends

        joining a banned
           communist trade union

    dropping leaflets
      like confetti
      from the top of the department store
      where they work

causing

                    quite a stir

making me burst
        with pride.

The doorbell

shatters the peaceful
quiet at home

ringing
        again and again and again

its urgency
making me step
out of the bathroom
        makeup brush in hand

its sound
shaking my parents
                to their feet
                to the door.

My brothers are out

I was about to leave myself

but as I step
in front of
Papa and Mama

I'm relieved I'm here
for them
          especially

because the ringing
is now accompanied
by a loud banging
on our door and

Papa and Mama share
a worried glance.
Papa nods and

I reach
for the handle

hoping whoever's on the other side
of the door won't mind
dealing with a petite, naive girl

because if anyone
can stand up to people
like this

it's
me.

RUFFIANS IN UNIFORM

The two of them take in
the three of us

on either side
of the threshold

neither daring
to cross

until they announce
my brother's name

Oskar
Pohorylle

direct their gazes
at my parents

wait glaring
as Papa pauses

says
my brother's not home

that we don't expect him
back anytime soon

to
which

they respond that it's fine
they'll take
me
instead.

SO KIND

They're kind enough
to allow me to collect
my things, put on
my coat and hat
       (fingers trembling the slightest bit)

       while they search the sitting room
              and my bedroom

kind enough
to allow me to kiss

my parents goodbye

       Mama frozen
       Papa's eyes filled with tears

before leading
me out the door
down the stairs
to the car that takes me to
       Gestapo headquarters.

PRISONER

Flash
       and I'm photographed

Smash
       and I'm fingerprinted

Shake
       and my pockets are emptied

and I'm patted down
gripped by the arm
led to a small room
for questioning.

The questions are
             short
             specific
             targeted

about my brothers and
my friends and
about me and what
I support and why
I don't support
                    national socialism

about other acquaintances
who might be responsible
for more serious

acts
of
treason

but I force myself to remain
calm and fearless

             playing the
                         innocent
                    female with a
                    wink and a smile

which they evidently find

unexpected
and soon I'm ushered
to a cell to wait
while they figure out
what to do
with someone
like me.

Time drags on

as I pace
a crowded cell filled
with other female prisoners
doing my best to cheer
everyone despite
the heavy fear and
foreboding hanging
over us all.

One missed Shabbat, two
but I hold up

      equal parts
           bravado and
           naivete

whenever they call
me to interrogations

giving
nothing
and no one
away

but by night
in the same cell
I'm unnerved
shaken
by the sounds

        screams
                shouts
                        cries

traveling through
the walls
and
the floors

clear evidence
that the male prisoners
are being
tortured

and that's it
        I've had enough.

Even if things seem fine
for us female prisoners

      they are not

           if they're not fine
           for others

and I can't keep on
as if they are.

Instead I step to the door
and ring the bell to
call the guards, shocking
my cellmates as I let
everyone know

I refuse
to stand
for this.

As usual

they have no idea
      what to do
           with the likes
of me
           and the result

of my alarm-sounding
is a sound scolding
a warning
not to touch that bell again
but at the very least
my point has been made
that my fellow prisoners do not
deserve
this treatment
and some people
won't let them get away with it.

APRIL 1933

SURPRISE

One morning
a guard comes
for me
and I can tell
from her resigned demeanor
that something is
different
and I stiffen
wondering if I've finally
gone too far.

But instead of leading
me to an interrogation
room, she leads me
back to the door
I entered
three long weeks ago.

They give
me my things
make me sign
a release

and
I'm allowed
to leave
this jail
       behind
for the civilization
of the street.

Relief

escapes my body in a
whoosh of pent-up
breath

once the door
clangs closed

behind me

sending me
back
into the world

the air warmer now
after my weeks inside
and

filled
with blossoming
          hope.

HOMECOMING

With my family
surely worried

          I speed for home

but the sound of
my heels clopping
up the stairs to the flat
is enough to alert
them to my return

and I reach the open
doorway to find
my parents'
anxious expressions
waiting for me
my brothers'
relieved faces
behind them

and they pull me inside
where we cling
to each other

      praising
      God

we're together
once again.

THE POLISH CONNECTION

I tell them
how glad I am
to be back home
and they share a glance
before Papa tells me

We asked a Polish diplomat
to intercede on your behalf.

Mama adds

We had no idea if he'd be
successful, but we had hope.

My parents!
So resourceful!
I grin.

Though I was born
        in Germany
my passport has been
                Polish
since the Great War ended

and I would never
have thought
it would help
in times like these

but it was evidently
fortuitous for me
now relaxing
in my living room
surrounded by
those I love.

When I ask

What did I miss?

the question is enough
to make everyone's smiles
disappear.

DARK TIMES

I can tell before anyone
says a single word
that something terrible
has happened.

*It's going to be harder
for me to do business.* Papa sighs.
*There's been a boycott
and several new laws.*

Oskar wordlessly hands me
the papers from the
past few days, and I pore
over the headlines.

MARCH 29

BOYCOTT ORDERED

CALL TO ACTION BY NATIONAL SOCIALIST LEADERS

MARCH 31
IMPLEMENTATION OF
THE BOYCOTT
BY THE NATIONAL
SOCIALIST
DEFENSE COMMITTEE

And no one has
to tell me
    the target
of this boycott was
      us Jews.

    But it's over now?

        It was a one-day boycott, Mama says.

        It was, Papa says,
        but it set a dangerous precedent.

Oskar points out the text
farther down on one of the papers
describing how the nazi-led boycott
would be implemented.

This of course concerns businesses
owned by members of the
Jewish race.
Religion is irrelevant.
Jewish business owners
baptized as Catholic or Protestant
are also Jews.

And although it's over
for now

it's also clear that
this country's new government
won't tire of pushing us around

making my eyes narrow
making my hands form fists
making me more than ready
to fight.

PLANS

I push my anger aside and
pool my positivity
before asking my question

keeping my voice
                bright.

        So what are we going to do
                        about this?

Once again, they share
a glance, my unshakable parents
        afraid.

                        I've already begun
                                liquidating
                        the business, Papa says quietly,
                        so they can't take it away.

                        We'll do our best
                                to stay afloat,
                                Mama adds,
                        but after your arrest . . .

Another glance
this time shared
with my brothers
and my breath freezes
        trapped
in my throat.

                        We think it's best
                        if you leave Germany,
                                Papa says.

The seconds tick
by on the clock as
the words sink in.

Without you?

And the very idea fills
me with a rush of emotions

above all

a fair heap of fear
and not for me
leaping into the unknown

but for them
staying here

behind.

SNAPSHOT

Oskar and I retreat
to a quiet corner of the flat

where I'm still struck
by the sights, sounds, smells of home

a home I'm in
no hurry to abandon

so I cross my arms
wait for Oskar to speak.

Look, Papa won't rest until
you're somewhere safe.

But what about them?
What about you?

They'll make it work somehow.
And Karl and I will help them.

But I could stay
and help too.

Oskar reaches for my arm
shakes his head.

Now that you've been arrested
you won't get off so easy next time.

And before I can respond
Karl joins us
his expression resolute.

Oskar and Karl

convince me
      they'll lie low
convince me
      they'll protect our parents
convince me
      everything will be fine.

DESTINATION

Once it's decided
I run through my list
of contacts to figure out
the best place to go.

Georg is off studying
in Italy
and moving there
      or back to Stuttgart with
           Meta or Pieter
wouldn't help
get me out
from under fascists
anyway

but

Ruth has been talking
about Paris
is already planning
to head there soon

so there's nothing that
makes more sense

than for me to
leave Leipzig
stop in Stuttgart
proceed to Paris
myself

a single girl
needing
solo escape.

SEPTEMBER 1933
FAMILY LIFE

After months of
preparations

discussions
plans

my moment of departure
has arrived
and as I snap
my suitcase shut
look around this flat
      my home for
      the past four years
I can only pray
it will continue
to safely harbor
my family
without me.

I try to hold in
      an avalanche of anxiety for them
          and
      my growing excitement
          for myself
and focus
on these four dear people
      Papa
      Mama
      Oskar
      Karl

as I embrace them

hold them close to my heart
in this last moment together
in our
home sweet home.

SNAPSHOT

Our walk to the train station
is uneventful

a strange sense of the inevitable
hanging over us   like rain clouds

and though I expected
Papa

would be the most inconsolable
(it's no secret I'm his favorite)

it's in fact Mama
a wetness filling her eyes

as if she suspects
she'll never see

her daughter again

who moves me to tears.

OLD FRIENDS

On the way to Paris I stop
in Stuttgart, where
Meta brings me to her home

and its relative safety
where we spend
          hours, days, over a week

together
and it's as lovely as
ever being together

being welcomed by her family
even seeing Pieter
          now a dear friend

and the two of them make sure
I have enough money
to get on my feet in Paris

but I decide it's better
to keep the reason
I had to flee

          to myself.

UNWANTED NEWS

My decision to keep
some secrets seems
like a good one when
Meta is less than enthused

about the leaflets I pull
            out of my suitcase
about my plans
            to fight fascism

less willing
to believe in

my insistence
            that the situation in Germany
                        is only going to
                  get worse
            for people like me

and her silence
to my alarm bell
is deafening.

ON MY OWN

Once the train departs
      Stuttgart for Paris
slowly chugging
westward, leaving
my former life
my run-in with
      the Gestapo
          behind

I allow myself
the luxury of enjoying
the journey

      wide-eyed and
         full
      of anticipation

for my future and
my newfound
independence.

THE CITY OF LIGHTS

It's a long trip into
          France
and I'm finally growing
weary the farther I get
from home until
the landscape gives way

      to buildings sprouting
      closer together in
      bigger and taller clumps

making me sit up
zoom in on my surroundings
count the minutes
until they announce
our arrival at

      Gare de l'Est
            of this dazzling city:
            Paris.

SNAPSHOT

Ruth is ready and waiting
for me, wearing
a stylish dress
an enthusiastic smile
even a jaunty beret
over her lovely locks

      and I snap a photograph
            in my mind
      a souvenir of this moment.

We embrace
kiss each other's cheeks
      ooh la la
and she sweeps
me away to a
friend of a friend
who offers a place to stay
until I find a job

which I'm determined
will be
      as soon as
           possible

because now that I'm free
from the Reich's iron grasp
I'm ready

      to parler, sourire, flirter

my way into this city's
               heart.

A NEW STRUGGLE

At first being here
is a deep breath held
        full of hope

and I don't even think
about anything else
as I take in
        these historic streets
                these bustling cafés
                        these elegant people

but

after a couple of days
the glitz dims
excitement dims
my optimism dims

as I realize
it's going to take
all my efforts

to find a way
to survive

in a city
                    teeming
with other refugees
            eyes full of hope
just like
mine.

SIMILARITIES AND DIFFERENCES

I don't mean to compare
            but having lived in two German cities
                    and one small Swiss town

I can't help but fall
for this cosmopolitan city
            bigger than anywhere
            I've ever been

                    boasting
                            chic women wrapped in furs
                                    shopping, dining, strolling
                            men in suits and hats
                                    dapper in broad daylight

but

while there are no
obvious boycotts here
like there were in Germany

it's still obvious
       Parisians prefer their own
             over us.

Liebe Familie

Just a quick note
to let you know I've
settled in

and to tell you that Paris
is a destination
you should definitely consider.

       I'd help you with the French!

Please write me
with all your
news.

SLEEPING ARRANGEMENTS

I see them everywhere I go
      in public parks
            alleys

people who can't scrape
together the money
to pay for a bed

and I feel for them
because I'd be sleeping in
the park myself without
Ruth's friend's divan and
the money that both
Meta and Pieter
so kindly gave me

so in the meantime
I save every centime I can
for the future flat
I aim to share with Ruth

our base for
making this city
our own.

MAIS OUI

I have it much better
than most
with my years of studying
now flawless French

which allows me to blend
in among the crowd

and though I can't get
official permission to work
      being a foreigner
at least a world of
black market jobs
is available to me

because I fit in
      a fausse Parisienne.

Ruth and others make do
as servants, cleaners, seamstresses

but it doesn't take long
for me to find an off-the-books
position as a secretary

and just like that
my foot's in the door.

HEADLINE

Part of the pleasure
of spending time at a café
is poring over the papers
people pass around
but this week's news
out of Germany
is cause for concern.

REICH REPORTERS LOSE

LAST OF THEIR RIGHTS

MUST SERVE STATE

HEAVY PENALTY SET FOR

ARTICLES PENNED AGAINST NAZIS

WITH DEATH FOR TREASON

The one thing
everyone here
        Parisian or refugee
can agree on is that

freedom of the press
is essential
for any free country

while at the same time it's clear
that freedom is something
my former country
can no longer claim.

SHOEBOX

Ruth and I finally find
a cheap room to share
on the border of
the Thirteenth
and Fourteenth
Arrondissements

not at all far from the
Quartier Latin
Jardin du Luxembourg
cafés de Montparnasse

places we'll be spending
our free time

because there's only enough

space for
sleeping
here

and with a
drill sergeant of a landlady

the outside world is
exponentially
more pleasant
anyhow.

DAY OF REST

Just like in Germany
everything shutters down

on Sundays
in France

and now that it's getting cold
Ruth and I stay in

huddled under
our blankets

reading
resting

conserving
energy

for the week
ahead.

MEANWHILE

Fridays in France
mean
       assimilation

so even though
I have plenty of
Jewish friends here

      in fact I have very few
           who are not

none of us
      attends synagogue
           observes Shabbat
      betrays any sign of Anderssein.

Even when surrounded
by people
on Fridays I ache
for home.

SNAPSHOT

Near the end of December

    carolers parade the streets
    piping soft tunes in clear voices
    of bells and angels and Jesus

while people stroll home
    with secret packages
        and sweet smiles

making my chest ache
with longing for
my family.

OUR LIVING ROOM

Because our room is
too tiny for guests
      a problem we share
      with most fellow refugees

Ruth and I congregate instead
in the cafés

stretching out a
single coffee for
      hours

grabbing two croissants
from the counter, each
immediately devouring half
so it only looks like
we took one

feeling so grateful
to be where we are

as we chat, smoke, sip
the morning
away.

HEADLINES

This week's papers
paint a bleak picture of the
political upheaval
between the left and right
that's spread to France:

> PARIS MOBS ASSAULT LEGISLATIVE CHAMBER
> PLACE DE LA CONCORDE AND ELYSÉE
> PRINCIPAL POINTS OF BLOODY ENCOUNTERS

then

> AFTER THE RIOT
> CABINET RESIGNS

followed by

> COALITION CABINET FORMED

and though it's a coalition
of various parties
from the center and right
the government excludes
those from the left

and the only good thing
to come of that
is the realization
that the parties on the left
must come together on their own
to have any hope of success
in the future.

OPPORTUNITY SEEKER

At my secretarial job
                my fingers tap, tap, tap
        over typewriter keys
                    my eyes observe
                          all manner of visitors
           my ears take in
                    conversations
perking up
        when any potential opportunity
                presents itself
because I'm ready
        to jump
                on anything.

INFESTATION

As if our run-down room with its
        paper-thin walls
        sink we can never
               get clean
and
terrible landlady
weren't awful enough
        already

I wake up with
bug bites all over my
        legs, arms, torso
wake up itchy and sore and
irritable, glance
at Ruth.

        You too?

We're forced to spend
the entire morning scrubbing
every surface clean
scratching like mad

        and

we realize
that things
can always
get worse.

Liebe Gerda

Please note
the new address
on the envelope!

Yes, we've moved again
    a different neighborhood
    a different flat
but still together, we four.

No need to worry
about us.

But on the back
a scribbled note
from Oskar clues me in

    that they've been forced to move
    that the new flat is one room
    that things in Germany
        are becoming dire indeed.

FEELINGS

I'm filled with equal parts

        anger
over the injustice of this system
edging my family out

        worry
that they might not be able
to stay afloat much longer

        guilt
that I was able to escape
but they haven't

                        at least not yet

and though they'll probably
brush me off again

my response begs
above all my papa to consider
other places

where they might

find dreams
to chase.

PEN PAL

In between my hours at
      the office, cafés, home

I keep up on my
      correspondence
with friends from back home as well.

Meta and Pieter write
me notes filled with
a bit of cash each month

      though they both seem to think
      that things will blow over
      in Germany soon

      and

Georg sends me
invitation after
invitation to
visit him in Italy

and I finally consent
take a short trip
and it's lovely there
       sunny and warm and carefree

but it isn't Paris
with my growing circle
of friends
       people very much like me
so I kiss him goodbye, hop
on the train back, write
another
letter.

REFUGEES

Ruth and I meet
loads of people at the cafés
new friends and old
many of them
Germans in exile
       like us

including

Willi Chardack
a friend from Leipzig

along with authors and
artists and political
acquaintances
who've fled Germany for
        obvious reasons

who want as much as we do
to make sure
the dark nazi stain

doesn't spread
further.

The obvious reasons

for this wave
                of exile
come up in almost
                every new conversation.

Why did you *leave?*
                        Jewish.
                Communist.
                Anti-fascist.

And indeed most of us
are some combination

of the three.

Every time we discuss the situation
            our somber expressions speak for us
so we don't even
                have to say
what little hope we hold
                that it will blow over
                        anytime soon.

APRIL 1934

TOUGH TIMES

In the end I don't know
if it's me or the state of
the state in Paris

        where they're
        getting more hostile
        toward foreigners
        saying we're stealing
            French jobs

but the only thing
that really matters
is the outcome:

I'm sacked

which means
soon I'll be
hungry
penniless
desperate
once again

so I take the only
action I can

set my beret
on my head

head out there
          again.

ODD JOBS

I guess I should have
thought it through better
before choosing France
for my future

because now I'm having
trouble finding something

anything
to replace my income

and as my wardrobe gets
                    shabbier
and my stomach
                    emptier

I realize I won't be able to talk
my way out of this fate, so

I finally take on
a job I never thought I'd do

                    walking the streets

            my arms full of newspapers

making full use of
my bright smile
my language skills
as I call out
        Pariser Tageblatt!
                New York Herald!
                        Paris-soir!
and it's not much
but at least it's almost
            enough
to keep me

from starving
for the moment.

FASHION MODEL

Pretty as people say
      I am
and pretty positively
matters in Paris

I only like to use
my looks together with
                my wits
to get ahead.

Ruth on the other hand
      pretty in a completely
           different way

has begun making use of
what the nazis tout
as Aryan ideals
      athletic build
      blond hair
      blue eyes

has begun making a living

as a model
for any publication that asks

and luckily for me
she doesn't mind
covering a bit more
of the rent

when I come up
          short
two months
in a row.

GETTING BY

For the rest of the spring
and summer

we make do
pooling our earnings

collecting whatever help
our friends send

trying to figure out
how to put ourselves

on firmer

footing

trying to get ourselves
beyond survival

with the world shifting
beneath our feet.

AUGUST 1934
HEADLINE

We pass around the papers
raising our voices
in dismay

not so much at the news that

    PRESIDENT HINDENBURG

        DIED THIS MORNING

but at the news that

    HITLER BECOMES

    PRESIDENT OF THE REICH

    WHILE REMAINING

    CHANCELLOR

and that's it

the power of the party
is now

    absolute.

Liebe Familie

There's no denying
any longer
that the nazis
are in Germany

    to stay.

Please let me know
if you're thinking
of emigrating
and what I can do

    to help.

A GIRLFRIEND'S DUTY

I'm back in the room
feet up
after selling newspapers
all morning

    when

Ruth appears
        breathless.

                I need you to come with me.

And she knows
as well as I do
that I will never
turn her down
not after everything
she's done for me
so I only ask

    Where to?

as I straighten
my dress, lace up

my shoes

        game

for anything.

ON THE WAY

Ruth fills me in
about the photographer
who approached her
at La Coupole
      one of our favorite
         cafés

telling her he needed
a model with just her look
for some pictures
he wanted to take
of her in a park

and while Ruth welcomed
the idea of being photographed
      as usual
her alarm bells rang
at the idea of being
alone anywhere
with this mysterious man

and so
she told him she'd meet
him at a small park
in Montparnasse
      only
if she could bring
a friend along

       (me).

UNEXPECTED

Ruth's photographer is
so intently studying something
through his camera's viewfinder
that he doesn't even notice
us approach at first

but Ruth nods, points, tells me

That's him.

Only then does he lower
the camera, look
our way, break
into a smile

and the world seems to

pause

for a moment
as I take in this
dark-haired, dark-eyed handsome thunderbolt of a man

and when our gazes meet
sparks pass between us
electric.

Ruth marches
toward him, presents
us to each other

André Friedmann
Gerda Pohorylle

and even after Ruth shakes
his hand in a proper
Germanic hello

André and I wordlessly agree
to greet each other with a
bisou, bisou
on both cheeks

perfectly
Parisian

(though we're both clearly
anything but)

and
perfectly
in
tune

with each other.

STUDENT AT WORK

I observe
from the sidelines
as André instructs Ruth

where to stand
how to position herself

paying attention as he studies
natural light
unexpected angles

(things Meta's Onkel Friedrich
didn't seem to consider
back then)

and I'm as surprised
as intrigued

with the way
this scrappy yet charming man has
seemingly mastered
the art of photography.

SNAPSHOT

The shutter clicks
grounding me
in this moment
and it's so captivating
that all I want to do
is hold
my own camera
look through
my own viewfinder
myself.

AU REVOIR

André snaps the last shot
                click
                        advances the film
                                whirr
thanks Ruth for her time
            and she and I turn to leave
                        but
before we've taken two steps
                he calls out
                                    Wait!
        speeds to my side
                    dives into my eyes
                            asks when he can
                                    see me again.

PLANS

We decide to meet
at La Coupole

        the café where he first
                met Ruth

as if tomorrow
                can't come
        soon enough

but

I already have a date
with Willi tomorrow

        and André's calendar is
                booked the following day

so we reluctantly decide
to leave our next meeting
up to
fate.

OCTOBER 1934
BONJOUR

A month later
the afternoon sun hangs
low over Paris as I hurry

toward a café to meet
some friends

stopping momentarily
at the newsstand
        distracted
by one of the headlines

        CABINET QUITS IN SPAIN
        NEW REVOLT FEARED

and something stirs
in my heart but
I push it aside to
speed ahead and find
I'm the first one
to make it.

However, instead of my
circle, to my surprise
I see *him*

      on the terrace
           at a table for two
                    sitting with
              an empty seat
                    for one.

CHARMANT

André stands
his face lit up
with a bright smile
brown eyes twinkling

as he takes a step
toward me around the table
his arms enveloping me and

     bisou, bisou

his kisses fall
soft as snowflakes
on my cheeks.

Please, you must join me.

He pulls out my chair
offers me a cigarette
raises a finger to summon
the waiter
asks me to tell him
        everything
about myself

and our exchange
begins.

CALL-AND-RESPONSE

I tell him all about
the places I've lived
what brought me to Paris
my family, my friends

and he breaks up my tales
with stories of his own
growing up in Hungary
          in a Jewish family

with a pause
after that last admission
just waiting for me to confirm

          me too

before launching into
his struggles to stay afloat as
a freelance photographer
in Paris while unable
to master French

and I smile
at his charming accent

especially when he tells
me there's something
he thinks we share

    a hunger
    a passion
    a drive

to do something big
              in this world

and I can tell
my eyes are sparkling
at the joy of finding
a friend who feels
      exactly
the same way.

NOVEMBER 1934

A LITTLE ROMANCE

As much as I enjoy
my growing friendship
      with André

I'm not made
for one person only
and in fact I enjoy
the company of
countless
others

including Willi
            something more
                        than a friend
            at the moment

Pieter
            who comes
                        to Paris
            for a short visit

and Georg
            receiving me once more
                        in Italy as a visitor

each of them offering
just what I need
            precisely
when I need it.

BOUNCING AROUND

Beyond the boys
Ruth of course remains
one of my dearest friends

even after
I decide
to move out

swapping homes
from one friend to
another

like an escargot
leaving its shell
        behind.

BOUNDARIES

With our busy schedules
it's a while until
André and I can see

each other again

and when we do
this time at
     Café du Dôme

we make eye contact
across the room

       his gaze lit brighter
       than a shooting star
          dangerous

himself, hurtling toward me
with open arms.

We greet with a
         bisou, bisou
our lips lingering
on each other's cheeks

      ever so close

but with my heart
already swelling
from those stars
in his eyes

I need to stop myself

fast
from falling
because

this is a line
I'm not ready
to cross.

After all

I've been engaged
        before
and I know as well as anyone
that
something this
                electric
can only mean
        trouble.

Especially

because as attracted
as I am to André

        (and I'll admit that
        to no one but myself)

                        I can't help but notice the way

his camera

his most prized
possession

keeps ending up in hock
at the pawnshop

so he's certainly not
the most eligible catch

even if
I wanted to catch him.

And yet

the more time I spend
with André
the more I realize
that I seem to have met
the male version
of myself

and I like
this male version
of myself

and although I don't want
to tie myself down

to anyone or anything
        at least not right now

I'm certainly not willing
to let this extraordinary bond
        fizzle out
so even when we're apart

I keep our connection
very much alive
as a possibility
in my heart

        and it's easy

knowing
he's doing exactly
the same.

APRIL 1935

Liebe Gerda

*Things have quieted down
    have stabilized
and we're going about
our business in Leipzig*

all settled in our

neighborhood
flat
home

and we only hope
you're doing as well
as the four
of us.

NEW FLATMATE

The past months have been
      a whirl
of activity

moving from place to place
scrambling for cash
         every day
getting to know André's friends
Chim and Henri
     fellow photographers
     who capture
      people, places, politics
trying to set goals
     beyond tomorrow

but things finally settle
when I land in the flat of

fellow refugees
Fred Stein and his wife, Lilo.

Not only does Fred help
me out by slipping me back
some of the cash I give
him for rent

but since he can no longer
practice law
he's making a living now
as a photographer and has set up
the flat's bathroom
as a darkroom

      a darkroom!

and with this opportunity
presenting itself
right in front of me
           like fate

I ask and
he agrees
to teach me
      everything
he knows.

TOP STUDENT

Out on the street
I watch Fred shoot
with his compact Leica

      learning
how to bear witness
      to even the most mundane
            of moments

      taking notes
to submit as newspaper captions
in whichever language
          Fred needs.

Back in the flat
I'm soon soaking up

how to
mix
      chemicals with water
shake
      rolls of film
soak
      special paper in baths

as what we just witnessed
              in real life

slowly takes shape
before our eyes
          in print.

DARKROOM

Fred doesn't mind
André coming over

developing prints
with me

and André's deep, charming voice
gives me further instruction

about deepening contrast
making use of shadow.

It's close quarters in here
all elbows and stepped-on toes

fumbling in this darkness
our cheeks lit up
                exposed

under the
single
red
bulb.

SNAPSHOT

It's the most natural
thing in the world when
André's arm wraps
around my waist

our breaths
      held

our eyes
      unblinking

          un, deux, trois

until

our lips
    slowly
       carefully
meet

and my heart!

Nothing
will ever
be the same

    again.

COMPARING KISSES

After having kissed
        André
    I realize
that although kissing others
      is still
        somewhat fun
somehow
     my heart's
        not with them
   but with
him.

REPORT

Once spring arrives
André heads off to Spain

on assignment
and I can just imagine

being somewhere
on assignment

and I love hearing
all the details in his letter

capturing important
moments there

from a balloonist reaching new heights over Madrid
to the festivities of Semana Santa in Sevilla

anecdotes that animate
me even more

to cultivate my own craft until
I see the letter's unexpected

last
lines.

POSTSCRIPT

I love adventuring
around Spain

aventuras
en España

but I miss Paris
and your arms and

sometimes
I even think

I'm falling
in love

with you.

PLANS

André's romantic confession
from so far away
is unexpected

though not unwelcome

and my heart stirs
with the thrill of
possibility.

But I'm too busy with
      my scramble for cash
            work, work, work
      my new interest in French politics
            with the formation of the anti-fascist
                  Front Populaire
                  an alliance of left-leaning movements
      my thirst for knowledge
            throwing all my extra centimes
                at my new hobby
to dwell on my feelings.

When I meet Willi
one day at La Coupole
      no longer another romantic entanglement
      but simply a good friend

and he proposes
a summer trip
to the south of France
with him and another friend
to get away from it all

I decide
to give it some
serious
thought.

ENCOURAGEMENT

One night over a dinner of
baguette and brie
with Fred and Lilo

I bring up
Willi's offer
still unsure myself

and

the two of them take
one look at each other
before nodding and smiling.

We were hoping . . . Lilo begins

. . . *you might*
take a break someday, Fred finishes.

They go on to tell
me that they'll hold

my room for me

that they'll be
here for me

that I should take
this opportunity.

AUGUST 1935
ESCAPE

I make the rounds
to various cafés telling
friends

> *au revoir*

and

> *à bientôt*

give Fred and Lilo
firm hugs and kisses

shoulder a small rucksack

> no need for a full suitcase
> for a few weeks

of summer fun

and hurry off
to meet the boys.

ON THE ROAD

Willi and his friend Raymond
are the jolliest of companions
when the first ride we hitch rattles south

away from city pollution
and toward
fresh seaside air

and I'm pleased
to be traveling
with them

but secretly I'm
even more excited
about the possibility

in the latest
telegram
from André

that he's going to try

to get to Cannes
to meet me.

CANNES, FRANCE
A DIFFERENT WORLD

Stepping off the back
of our last ride

      a delivery truck
      that drops us
      at the coast

is like nothing I've
ever experienced

because

even if my pockets hold
barely enough cash
to keep me afloat

I'm on a real vacation
away from
the hustle and the
      pressure
to keep up

and this alone
is the best gift
I've ever given
myself

and the best
I've ever
received.

THE NEXT DAY

André arrives
and I can barely believe
he's here too
that we're both here

      in this sea-salt air
          and singsong sunshine

that we can escape the world around us

      and dive
           into each other
     instead.

SNAPSHOT

His cheeks are scratchy
           his eyes hungry
                     lips soft
            and when we wrap ourselves up
                       in each other
           my heart captures
                 the flash
           between us
shining bright
      in the dark.

SAINTE-MARGUERITE, FRANCE
OUR OWN NEVERLAND

The lot of us takes a ferry
to the island of
Sainte-Marguerite
where we live
as cheaply as possible

       eating baguettes
       and tinned sardines

listening to ocean waves
watching stars twinkle
       as the sky turns to night

sleeping in tents

       Willi and Raymond in one
          André and I in another

and a part of me wishes
a life like this
could go on and on

       for infinity

like the tides
          bringing
wave after wave
onto these shores.

COMPARISONS

One evening
over a cheap vin de table
and fresh-caught crab
       the shellfish a first
       for both me and André

the two of us swap stories
about our upbringings
     middle-class
     trying to fit in
     two brothers.

So similar!

          But I spent more time away
          from home than in it, he begins,
          running around Budapest with
            friends
            girlfriends.

He waggles his eyebrows
     making me laugh
asks to hear my own adventures

so I decide to dig deeper
tell him the tale of Meta's students
and their antisemitism
and how I had to keep my mouth shut
         and hide
my Jewishness
to which André laughs
a bitter laugh.

         There's no hiding this.

He points to his face
and I reach for his rough cheek
glad he'll never have to
hide his true self

from me.

SNAPSHOT

Only now do I realize
that as much as I enjoyed
getting out of the home
as a teenager

I also cherished
my moments
in it

and when the first star
appears in the night sky
it burns bright
as a Shabbat candle
in my heart

my own shimmering memory
of home.

WHO WE ARE

Next André shares
something else softly, quietly
as if sure the words will drive me away.

> *I don't even know if I can ever*
> *return to my homeland.* He pauses.
> *I was arrested for my politics.*

In a flash
I'm back
in the cold Leipzig jail

and I shudder
but André doesn't notice
keeps talking.

> *It was quite traumatic*
> *police officers pounding me*
> *my father requesting my release.*

I wince.
Those terrible sounds
traveling through the walls.

André wraps an arm around me
as if to comfort me
for his past trauma

his arm falling
when I share
         my own.

Once again
our lives
so similar.

OUTDOOR CLASSROOM

By now André is familiar
with my never-ending thirst
to learn more

         about everything in general
         but photography in particular

and while he's already impressed
with my darkroom skills

he agrees to make the island
my classroom, teaching me more

and soon I'm learning
everything there is to know about

composition
camera angles
light exposure

and each day that I take
his camera in my hands
it feels more like

an extension
of me.

TRUE CONFESSIONS

After a few weeks
of this near-perfect paradise

I finally admit
(to myself)

that I might indeed be
falling
in love

with this magnet of a man whose pull on me
is no longer deniable

and even if

I will always be
my own person
first

I might actually
be willing to share
my deepest heart

with
him

so under the stars that
night, when he tells me

                              Je t'aime. Je t'adore.

I finally, quietly
            confess
my love
right back.

CANNES, FRANCE
SEPTEMBER 1935
HEADLINE

We don't often
visit the mainland
but one day we do

and we head to the newsstand
hungry for the world
beyond the island

but seeing the words in black and white
in the *New York Herald Tribune*
stuns us to silence.

REICH ADOPTS

SWASTIKA FLAG

OUTLAWS JEWS

We read on to learn about
new laws announced
in Nuremberg

banning Jewish-German marriages

depriving German Jews

of citizenship

making me think of Pieter
and how our union would now
be illegal

making me think of my family and me
luckily no longer German
but Polish.

Though all of us left Germany
primarily
for politics

it seems the time to flee
for the rest of our family and friends
has come.

Liebe Familie

I've just seen the papers
with these ludicrous new laws
and I know
they don't affect you

with your Jewish–Jewish marriage
and your Polish citizenship

but these are surely signs

of worse things to come
so I hope you're preparing
to emigrate soon.

It's not like

the French love
people like us

but at least
those in charge

here aren't
trying to steal

our basic
rights.

PARIS, FRANCE
OCTOBER 1935
AUTUMN

With the chill in the air
       and in the world
we reluctantly gather

ourselves and our things
and return
to Paris

where my room at
Fred and Lilo's flat
still waits for me.

It's as cozy and homelike
as before

but

it doesn't change the fact
that I miss André

miss falling asleep
in his arms

and though neither of us
is ready for anything
serious

(I cringe, remembering
my teenage self
getting engaged on a whim)

we can't deny
any longer

that we belong
          together.

LANDMARK

André and I slowly, carefully
          investigate
rooms for rent in the city

find one just down the block
from La Tour Eiffel

and it's as tiny
as any room I've rented in Paris

but we blissfully decide
it'll do just fine

          blissfully sign the lease

from this moment
forward

          blissfully convinced

                    that everything
     will be perfect.

NEW LIFE

After André and I move in together

      I land a job
            at Alliance Photo
                  working for Maria Eisner
                        (one of André's connections)
            using my language skills
            while learning all I need to know
                  about the business
            in a professional, symbiotic
                relationship

and even André picks up
a steady part-time paycheck
as a photo editor

            but we still find time
            on the weekends
                to get out to the cafés
                to continue with my
                      photography lessons
                to follow our passion
                      producing freelance articles
                      together
                          his pictures

my text

to live life
to the fullest.

NEW LOOK

Last year
I dyed my hair red
with henna

perhaps unconsciously trying
to fit in here in fashionable Paris

making people think
of me as a fox

but

I decide I'm ready
to try something new
and go blond this time

surprising
everyone

providing me with

a thrill

even if it's only
    temporary.

IN CHARGE

André might jokingly
call me

          le chef
          (the boss)

but he knows as well as I do
that he needed a little
    polishing

    putting on a jacket and tie

      getting out there and earning
          a living

    projecting
a professional image

and he's the first to admit
that my fashion tutorials
are already contributing

to his newfound success
as a photojournalist

and he bursts with public pride
about this tiny firecracker
at his side
       (me)

and

about the successful couple
we seem to be on our way
      to becoming

           not simply surviving
              but thriving.

DECEMBER 1935
SURPRISE

After only two months
sharing the same tiny bed

in the same tiny room
we begin to grate

on each other's nerves
begin to get

in each other's way
starting with me

frustrated with André's
man-child behavior

        turning up late for a photo shoot
                losing out on a job

ending with him
frustrated with me

        parading around the flat
             in nothing more

        than a bra and a slip
        when guests stop by

(even male guests)
so the one thing

we agree on
is that we can use

some
        time
                apart.

NOT SWEET HOME

Without him there
I can barely look at

      the four walls
      the lone window
      the bed

                things that used to
          be ours

and though I wander
the city, visit
my favorite cafés, chat
and smile and laugh
with friends

there's no denying
the André-shaped hole
in my heart.

Liebe Gerda

Good news.
We've scraped together

enough funds

to leave the Reich

and though we're not
able to make it to France
we've told the Jewish social welfare office
that we'd be happy with any
destination
>*away*
>*from*
>*Europe.*

For now, we've secured
train tickets to Yugoslavia

to your grandparents in Petrovgrad
where the rest of the family
is gathering

>*not perfect*
>*but nevertheless*

>>*away.*

JANUARY 1936
NEW YEAR

At the annual festivities
        arranged by Willi
                I bump into André
and after an awkward
        first moment
we both surrender
             admitting that
        as hard as it was
             being together
it's even
             harder
        being apart
and we kiss
        our forgiveness
             our feelings
                our promises
        to try
again.

PARTNERSHIP

One of the first things
we admit

after wholeheartedly agreeing

we missed
each other's
    kiss
    smile
    touch
is that we both missed
    working together

a union that brings
us great joy

and an even
greater purpose.

A NEW GAME

Not unlike the game
we played at finishing school

one night before
we fall asleep

I decide to ask André
what he likes best about me

and he pauses, reaches
a soft hand to my cheek.

I like what everyone likes about you
    your smile
.   *your laugh*
    your confidence
    your cleverness.

But what I love about you is that
  all these things together
  make you the one unique Gerda.

And there in his response
I learn not only how he feels

about me but also how I feel
about him

the one unique
      André.

HEADLINE

News of the upcoming elections
in Spain electrifies

conversation after conversation
at Café du Dôme
especially when campaign posters

from the leader
of the right-wing CEDA party
paper Madrid
with the words

GIVE ME THE ABSOLUTE MAJORITY
AND I'LL GIVE YOU
A GREAT SPAIN

because
absolute power

is the furthest thing
from greatness.

DIVISION OF LABOR

Closer to home in Paris
we follow the news with
André shooting the photographs

me writing not just captions
but pitches and copy
in whichever

                    target language
        for whichever
                    publication

and

we both slip
into the darkroom

creating stories
            together.

FEBRUARY 1936
HEADLINES

At La Coupole we consider it
our duty to scan the papers
for signs of instability
anywhere in Europe

and there are plenty
        of signs

            BRITISH POLICY ON ITALY

            MAY END IN WAR,

            IL DUCE WARNS

HITLER TALKS PEACE
AS OLYMPIC GAMES OPEN
IN SNOWSTORM

RESULTS OF SPANISH ELECTIONS
GIVE THE ADVANTAGE
TO THE LEFTIST FRENTE POPULAR

giving our circle plenty
to discuss.

*It's sounds like Il Duce
is looking for an excuse.*

*Hitler might talk peace
but he's stoking the flames
as much as Mussolini.*

*At least the Frente Popular
seems to have captured control
in Spain.*

And we drain our cafés
expressions
worried, concerned,
hopeful.

OFFICIALLY OFFICIAL

I'm still working
at Alliance Photo

      trying to break in
      as an independent
      photojournalist
            at the same time

when I'm issued my first
            press pass
from the ABC Press Service
      an agency from Amsterdam

and my smile in
the photo on
the pass is
infectious

because with this pass
I can now report the news
      anywhere
            at all.

My dear grandparents

All's well here
and I hope
all's well there
                but

I'm still waiting
for word from
        my parents
        my brothers.

Please ask them
to let me know
when they've safely
                arrived.

WEEK BY WEEK

André and I both work
incredibly long days
dragging each other
out of bed in the mornings

welcoming each other

back

after getting things done
      working hard
            earning our francs

and even with steady jobs
we still scramble
at the end of the week
to pay for
      rent
      food
      heat

but the one thing I've learned is that
           living on the edge
         is what truly makes me feel

               alive.

DATE NIGHT

One Friday night after
a particularly tough week

we make the choice
between dinner or wine

and bring the bottle and a
baguette back to the room

where we sit on the bed
by candlelight

sharing sips
between kisses and laughter

and ideas
for the future

each one bigger
than the next.

INSPIRED IDEA

André suggests
sending me around the city
as his ambassador

If anyone can get my work published
it's you, boss.

I'm laughing so hard
I'm crying

droplets of wine
dribbling down the bottle
down my chin

and he kisses them
                away
drinking from my skin

until a new idea strikes
my brain like a match
flaming to life with
sudden ferocity.

> *What if I act as the ambassador*
> *for someone else?*

> *Someone famous?*

> *Someone used to getting paid*
> *handsomely*
> *for his work?*

Suddenly

we're not laughing
            anymore.

We both sit up

straighter

André sets the wine bottle
      on the ground

and I continue
painting a picture

of this mysterious photographer
whose work I represent.

        We'll come up with a name
           for him

        and nothing like our Polish and Hungarian
           names

        but something that sounds
           flashier

        something you'd hear in
           Hollywood

        something
               American.

BRAINSTORMING

We get out a notebook
take turns scribbling ideas

and eventually come up with
new names for the both of us

     Robert Capa

        and

     Gerda Taro

both without a clear origin
     though clearly
     not Jewish

and

both with plenty of
     star quality

perfect
for the pair

we aim
to become

and
like that

our transformation
is complete.

PARTNERS

SETTLING IN

It takes some time
to adjust to our new names
especially for me, trying to think
of the man I love

no longer as André
but as Robert

but he adores the way
I can make the name sound
> French
> German
> or even American

depending on the accent
I slather on it

and soon enough we're
> out there
trying to record history
> for the world.

FIRST STEPS

We start out with a plan to
bring Robert's work to
people and publications
we already know

and when I share
a set of photos with
Maria at Alliance

tell her all about
Robert Capa
a fantastic talent demanding
three times the going rate
for good reason

she takes one close look
says nothing

      but

her raised eyebrow
tells me she might not recognize
the art but she recognizes
          the artist

and it's evident we'll need
to widen our net.

SETTING UP SHOP

Robert and I move to a new room
at the Hôtel de Blois
closer to the Jardin du Luxembourg
install ourselves at the nearby
Café du Dôme

make appointments
                make plans

all the while paying
close attention
documenting both

the political situation
in France

        with the continued rise of the anti-fascist
                Front Populaire

        like the Frente Popular that just won
                elections in Spain

and the rise of Hitler's troops
       at Germany's border

suddenly at the forefront
         of conversation

            everywhere.

HEADLINES

The papers at Café du Dôme
include news in early March that

       GERMAN TROOPS HAVE ENTERED RHINELAND

       CHANCELLOR HITLER DENOUNCES

           VERSAILLES TREATY

and the next day that

          PARIS SCORNS HITLER'S OFFER

          APPEALS TO LEAGUE OF NATIONS

and the next that

            ENGLAND PLEDGES SUPPORT

            IF FRANCE IS ATTACKED

this while the people of France
speed toward their own
elections in May

but with the

REICH TO SPEED FORTIFICATIONS

ALONG BORDER

it appears
conflict
is looming
in the near future.

MORE HEADLINES

The news from Spain

though more distant
than the border with Germany

pulls our attention
with news that

PARTIES ON THE RIGHT

WILL WORK WITH THE GOVERNMENT

TO MAINTAIN PUBLIC ORDER

BUT SAY THEIR CANDIDATES
HAD MORE VOTES THAN
THE LEFTIST FRENTE POPULAR

and we stare at one another
wondering
how the defeated party
can make
such outlandish
        claims.

Liebe Gerda

We've arrived in Petrovgrad
and have moved in
with your grandparents
who send warm greetings.

I release a breath
I feel like I've been holding
for years

especially when I spot
Oskar's handwriting on the back
of the note.

We're already
        settled in
already working

already relieved
to be somewhere
more like home.

MAY 1936
PARADE

The first day of the month is
          May Day
marked in Paris by a gathering
at the Place de la République

and we head there with friends
Robert taking photos
me taking notes
for an assignment given
by Robert's friend Chim

to cover the Front Populaire
here in France
in these last days before
national elections.

The mood is electric
with an endless stream of
          demonstrations
          placards
          flags

people

all of them combining into
the beginning of an anti-fascist
wave that we pray
                    with all our hearts
will overtake France, Europe, the world

bringing with it
                            salvation
for us all.

SNAPSHOT

Out in the crowd
            scribbling furiously in my notebook
                            sometimes I spy Robert
                    the way his fingers focus, *click*, *whirr*
                    capturing everything I've just described
                                    in seconds
            with no need for words
and I take my own snapshot
        in my mind
        desperately wishing
                for a camera of my own.

SUCCESS

Suddenly it seems
like everything's going
our way

the Front Populaire wins
      the election here
just like the Frente Popular did
        in Spain

unions across the country
        organize
        strikes
to protest work conditions
to ask for better treatment
        better pay

and Robert and Chim head
to the Renault factory
to shoot exclusive photos

that I manage to sell
not by Friedmann
but by Capa.

It works until

we submit some photos to *Vu*
of police in Geneva arresting
a journalist

and the publisher
                    Lucien Vogel
telephones me
lets me know
he was in Geneva too

lets me know
that he knows
that Robert is André

                    (oops).

Even though he doesn't pay
as much as we demand

after some fast talking
we get the real prize

            photos published
                    in *Vu*

            with a line crediting
            them to Robert Capa.

BOOMING BUSINESS

Our partnership is blossoming
as is our business
and we rent a small studio
with a darkroom
together with Chim

and alongside the two of them
I too possess plenty
of ambition and now
                    finally
a clear goal

so even though I still spend
my weekdays working
at Alliance

I spend my weekends
borrowing whatever camera
I can get my hands on
        Robert's Leica
                or
            Chim's Rolleiflex

sharpening my shooting skills
making the camera in my hands

as important to me
as breathing.

JULY 1936
HEADLINE

SPANISH ARMY SEIZES MOROCCO
REVOLUTION SPREADS INTO SPAIN

My anti-fascist crowd
  at La Coupole talks
    of nothing else
because this military coup
    launched by
  a group of fascist Spanish generals
insurgent nationalists
    aiming to seize
      control
    of the country's Second Republic government
    who legitimately won the election
is the biggest news
  of the year.

DIGGING DEEPER

We pore over the papers
learn more about these

     insurgent nationalists
          military leaders who stand on the side of
               the exiled monarchy
               the Catholic church
               fascist Germany and Italy

     who seem to be
          counting on people's fear of
               communism
               socialism
               the left

     who are attempting to steal control from
          Spain's Second Republic
               which was legally voted into office.

Without saying anything
Robert and I agree
     to find a way there
          to see it
          to document it

to get involved in it

ourselves.

PREPARATIONS

The very next day
we begin

to get our affairs
in order

applying for the necessary
            papers

talking our way
into assignments

quitting our jobs
in a gamble

we know
we must take.

But

before we can leave
unexpected visitors roll
into town on the train

      Robert's mother
            and brother

who've left
Robert's gambling father
           behind
in Hungary

and while his brother
is pleasant

his mother is an
       overbearing
          bully

who tries to convince
Robert to go with them
across the Atlantic to
a new life in New York.

When I inform her

about our plans to head
for Spain, she takes
it as a personal affront

evidently deciding that I
am not the right girl
for her son

when I know better
than anyone that
it's not up to her
or me or
anyone else
to decide

but him.

In the end

we continue
    with our plans
        as they continue
            with theirs
        as I perhaps not-so-secretly hope
    we're two ships
passing in the night.

SHOPPING

I've managed to save
up enough cash to make
an important purchase
for the trip

      my very own camera

and while I consider
a Leica

      such a fantastic lens!
      such sharp pictures!

a Rolleiflex

      just like Chim's

in the end I choose
a 1935 Reflex-Korelle

      affordable yet
      top-notch

with a unique six-by-six format

that makes it matchless
for setting my own mark
on the world.

CAUTION BE DAMNED

I've always adored
traveling
especially someplace new
whether alone
or with friends or family

but

setting off on an adventure
like this with my
partner
lover
copain

despite the danger
we'll most certainly face

or perhaps
because
of it

sends a wave of courage
through my veins
making me feel

      wilder and more alive

than I've
ever felt
before..

Liebe Familie

Just a quick note
to tell you I'm off
to cover the conflict in Spain.

I'm glad
the four of you are
out of harm's way

and I'll do my best
to stay clear of trouble
      myself.

AUGUST 1936

FIRST FLIGHT

Lucien Vogel arranges
for the lot of us photojournalists

      including
      Robert
      me
      and Chim

to fly with him into Spain

      first time on an airplane!

and we're all filled with
boundless energy that surges
first when we step inside
      the little Lockheed
and then as we take off
rising up through
the bumpy air toward
the clouds.

It's breathtaking gazing
out the tiny window, observing
the patchwork fields that

give way to the Pyrenees

and we climb higher
over their white-topped peaks
until beginning a gentle descent
that suddenly

      changes

as the plane's nose
             plunges
toward earth
            accompanied by
a terrifying beeping
of an alarm
                  from the cockpit.

EMERGENCY

All joking and talking halt
as we passengers sit back and let
the pilots do their job

my short life
        inexplicably zooming
through my mind
Stuttgart, Leipzig, Paris

my family, Meta, Robert.

Will these moments be my last?

Robert squeezes my hand
while my heart squeezes
tight in my chest

and I'm not the praying type
but if I were, all I'd ask for
is more time

on
this
earth

because
I'm not
done yet.

CRASH

We slam into the ground
with incredible force
that sends us forward

then back

as the pilots struggle
to control this hunk of metal
breaking up around us sending

      people
      belongings
      metal fragments

into each other until
finally coming to
a roaring, creaking
stop

and we glance around
the wreckage
blinking
almost unable to believe
that we've all
      survived.

THE NEXT HURDLE

The pilots
      radio
for help

we've landed in a random field
after all and not
the airport

and Robert presses his lips
to mine
so very alive.

We check one another out
most of us miraculously
unscathed

and set our sights
on getting to Barcelona
our destination within reach

and though we're still too shocked
to say much about the disaster
we just survived

all of us know
we've used up
one of our lives

however many
we have left certainly
up for debate.

BARCELONA, SPAIN
MORNING

Things always look
better in the morning

and with Robert's smile
waking me warm

as the Spanish sun
streaming in the window

> his kisses
> even warmer

I'm ready to shake off
the bruises and aches

from our unexpected
bumpy arrival

ready to shake off
the nagging reminder

of my own mortality
lurking in my mind

ready to step out
of my chrysalis

unfurl my joie de vivre
and envelop

myself and these people
with possibility.

THE SPANISH REPUBLIC

Far away from the insurgent
        troops to the south
this northern city rises
to our window

its streets full
of crowds supporting
the
legitimate
government
of this
republic

        just like
                we do

making us toss the sheets aside

throw on our clothes
get ready like it's a race

and we give each other
a nod, grab
our cameras, head
downstairs and out
to the street

where the wave of
people we witnessed
from our window
swallows us

in a thundering swarm
of excitement

our cameras out and ready
to click and capture

everything.

The first thing I notice

once we're down
on the street
in the crowd
is how
for the first time

in my life I don't
     look
     seem
     feel
different
from everyone else
around me.

Here, I'm one of many
in a sea of brown-haired
everyday people
rather than surrounded by
blond Aryan giants or
fashionable French nationals

and already
I feel very much
part of something
much bigger than
any of us.

VIEWFINDER

The enthusiasm is
palpable, and simply walking
among these people
     as anti-fascist as me

rifles slung over shoulders
fists raised in the air

fills me

                  with raw energy
        that lifts me over the clouds
                         like a zeppelin

and when I look down
into the Reflex
I frame each shot
with unrivaled certainty
that I'm capturing
        history
with each and every
            click.

I can't help wishing

there had been a similar
      wave of support
           from the start
in Germany
               a counter-uprising
      from the people
                  telling those in charge

we don't want you in power
and we will fight you
for control
when the nazis
swallowed the last bits
of *our* republic.

But

I'm here now
and this isn't about us
but about these Spaniards who are
rising up
to support their republic
so I throw myself
in with them
prepared
to make their cause
my own.

FOLLOWER

All day long we follow
militia groups gathering
in ragtag formations

Robert and Chim and
Lucien scoping out
scoop after scoop

my own eye
leading me
to moments

I capture
with
my camera

of courage
of passion
of beauty

that show me
this battle is
worth fighting.

BEACH DAY

The next evening
we follow the masses
to the beach, where
groups of militia are
          assembling

in lines far from straight
without any sort of
          discipline

      nothing like
      the snap-to of
          nazi troops

      and probably nothing like
          the insurgent troops
          who launched the coup here
          either

but these volunteers' hearts
and minds
are all in

and watching these people
not only men
but also brave, determined
      women
ready to put their lives
on the line
for this cause

tells me that fascism
has no place
here.

TWO SIDES

We are David
to their Goliath

       small
       weak
       nothing

against

       strong
       confident
       gigantic

but like David
       we are filled with heart

so like David
          we are filled with

             hope.

SNAPSHOT

Most of the troops carry
rifles, but a militiawoman
holding a pistol
captures my attention

and when the rest of
her group breaks up
laughing and smoking
and relaxing

she takes aim
her unwavering gaze
facing an unseen enemy
her pistol level

and as she holds steady
ready to take her shot
I steal the moment, speeding
across the sand toward her

crouching down low
steadying my camera
focus, *click*, *whirr*

      breathe.

SHIPPING OFF

The next day we discuss
                        our plans
which all revolve around
getting to the front
seeing these troops
            take a stand

seeing them
head into action

                        so we start by heading to the station
                        snapping some shots of the
                                    unbridled enthusiasm
                                    on their faces
                                                poking out of
                                                train windows

                        ready

            so ready

and once the first wave departs
we hire a car
pack up

head for Aragón
in search of
glory.

FAILURE

The driver brings us
here
there
everywhere

but the actual front
        the action
remains as elusive

                as August rain
        over this dusty earth.

Instead

we get some shots
of soldiers waiting
half-heartedly training
digging in

        as barely a shot
        is exchanged

barely a battle
is begun

and after days of
ardor turned to
boredom we hop
back in the car

leave the quiet front lines
and head to the heart
of the country

Madrid.

MADRID, SPAIN
THE DEFENSE

After leaving the dusty plains
                    behind
we ramble through settlements that
grow bigger, more congested
the closer we get
to the city

until we're suddenly in
its midst, entering
its narrow streets

taking in

the sandbags piled up
by the government's republican troops
        aided by civilians
to keep insurgent nationalist forces
                out

the crumbling buildings
        evidence that
their bombs and artillery
have already hit the mark

and when our driver leaves us
at the Hotel Florida
right on Gran Vía

we enter
        ready
to record

                whatever
        lands our way.

SEPTEMBER 1936
MADRID

Bombs whistle and blast
through the night
leaving more damage in
their wake each morning

      gaping holes in facades
            broken glass in the street
        and sometimes
               slumped-over, unmoving
                  bodies on the ground.

Robert and I stop
bow our heads
silently remembering
the individual cost that comes
with this conflict

but in spite of the danger
      or perhaps because of it
we're even

      hungrier
         to show the world
      the true cost
         of war.

HEADLINE

While most of the headlines
in the papers here in Madrid
directly concern the conflict

    troop movements

        cities captured

today's news rattles me
so much that Robert asks me
what's wrong
so I point at the paper
translate the headline.

    THE ASSASSINATION OF
    FEDERICO GARCÍA LORCA
    IS CONFIRMED

I swallow.

    The poet, I say.

The insurgents
are assassinating
    poets

now

which tells me
all I need to know
about the enemy
        we're fighting.

THE FRONT

After spending several days
in a city under siege
we realize that
we need to get out

        bear witness
                to what it's like
                        on the ground.

We hire another car
pack up our belongings
head southwest toward
        Córdoba
where rumor has it
troops have amassed
on both sides

and by the time
we arrive

the fascists have
      already undertaken
      a great offensive

            all has already been
            lost

but when we visit
the headquarters at the rear
we find a gathering of
      inexperienced peasants
      fresh militiamen
after this first defeat

still ready

      to fight.

AN IDEA

Instead of heading
back to Madrid or
Barcelona or
Paris

Robert decides to make use of
the scene here
            already set

elaborate as Hollywood

gets permission from the
officers to follow the troops
in their exercises

as they jump
across trenches

as they run
over dusty fields

as they pretend
the enemy's on the
other side of that ridge

until real shots
are actually fired.

UNEXPECTED

The unmistakable

clacks and

pings

of rifle fire drill
into the air as we dive
back into the trench
where several young men
      surround me
      protect me
      hand me a helmet
while Robert raises
his Leica for a few
last shots.

The action subsides
in short order
but the results
of the skirmish
include not only our
first action but also

            unfortunately

      a very real
casualty

            a soldier who was alive
                  just moments ago

      snuffed out

human tragedy

that demands
that this individual
cannot have

        died

in vain.

SNAPSHOT

One moment here
     living, breathing
and in the next
       a still, unmoving
          corpse
shattered
over this dusty dry hot unforgiving landscape
     reminding me
       that every moment
         is fleeting.

NEXT STOP: TOLEDO

Shaken by what we've seen

        not a victory
            but a defeat

                        not triumph
              but death

Robert wordlessly wraps
strong arms around me
his beating, alive heart
              pressed
       against mine.

We load back up
into the car
leave this shattered village
           behind

head toward Toledo
where word is
a confrontation finally lies
on the horizon

filling us once more
                    with tentative, hesitant
        hope.

Along the way

we stop at the mines
of Almadén
where workers
are producing mercury
for the war effort

        although they stop hammering
                    long enough to raise their fists
                        for my photos

                        click, whirr
                        click, whirr

showing solidarity

as soon as I'm finished
they do their part
        joining
the republican cause
by going back
to work.

TOLEDO, SPAIN

Anticipation

sizzles through the
oven-like air on the
streets of Toledo

all sights pointed
at the looming
Alcázar

the fortress where
nationalist
insurgent troops

took control just
days after they launched
the coup back in July

where hundreds of
reporters now
congregate

waiting as our
republican militia
creeps closer

laying explosives

preparing to burst
their way through.

FIZZLED OUT

We wait
> keep waiting
> wait some more

along with all these other
> reporters
> photographers
> thousands of troops

but after several days with
> no movement
> no conflict
> no action

our time's run out
we need to head back
> to Paris
and as much as we don't
want to miss
a decisive moment

we both pray

for the sake of
this republic

that it comes
       soon.

SNAPSHOT

The last morning of
our last day in
Spain

I yawn, stretch, step
to the window
freeze.

          The Spanish land wakes warm
            under golden-pink rays
              of morning sun

      two boys play hide-and-seek
          ducking
      around corners, behind barrels

            the scent of fresh barras de pan
              rises up from the bakery below

and I *click, click* the moment
                    into memory
            with my mind
so deep inside it that
I don't even notice
Robert
            until
his arms surround
me, lips brushing
against my ear.

Regresaremos, mi amor.

I know he's right
know we'll return

                    but

I also know I'm leaving
a part of my heart here
in the red-hot center

        of Spain.

HOME

When Robert and I return
                    to Paris

we find that
our photos from
the first half of our trip
have already been published

            in *Vu*, of course
                    as well as *Regards*

from the rolls of film
we sent back

and we pore
over the issues
from the end of
            September

                    astounded

by the spreads we see
on the pages
of these
magazines.

Especially the one

in *Vu*
from September 23 with
two of Robert's photos from
the Córdoba front
    from that day when
        gunfire erupted

now part of a report
on militiamen titled

     CIVIL WAR IN SPAIN:

     HOW THEY FELL

     HOW THEY FLED

showing

a soldier's arms spread
            wide
    rifle
    in hand

as he falls backward

the man struck
    by a bullet

in that very moment

and Robert goes white
as we grip each other's hands
            remembering.

SNAPSHOT

It's as if
            you can see
                        the soldier's life
            leaving him
                                    floating
                        suddenly carefree
the moment
            the bullet stopped
                        his heart.

TO THE DARKROOM

We wordlessly develop
our latest rolls ourselves

and see other powerful
            things

even on the negatives
more dramatic than we
expected

scenes of
the spirit of the republic

the unequaled wholeheartedness
of the underdog

captured
by our lenses

the determination
and grit
of its people
to hold on to their country

and we hurry to make prints
submit our latest pieces

share this anti-fascist fight
with the world.

CATCHING UP

Finally caught up with work
a mountain of correspondence

overwhelms us

      letters from my family
      still doing well
         in Petrovgrad

         countless notes
         from Robert's mother and brother
            set up here in Paris
            at the Hôtel de Blois like us
            just one flight upstairs
         until their emigration paperwork
              to America
            comes through

     one from Georg
        asking me (tempting me)
        to visit him in Italy

and we roll up our sleeves
divide and conquer

        me with pen and paper

Robert running to his mother

     and as marvelous as it's been
     the two of us together these past months

I wonder if

this might be a good point
        to spend a little time

            apart.

NEXT PLANS

The latest news out of Spain
dominates headlines
even here in France.

      ON THE FRONT AT MADRID

      THE BATTLE RESUMES

          THE FALL OF MADRID EXPECTED

             IN THREE DAYS

Robert's ready to return
        right away
to cover
the republican defense
           of Madrid

and I'm torn

because

I want to go too

torn because

>   I don't want
>   to miss anything

but at the same time

>   I don't want
>   to witness
>   the fall
>   of another republic.

NAPLES, ITALY
NOVEMBER 1936

FREEDOM

All those years ago in Leipzig
when I first met Georg
I remember feeling
like I had to choose

between him

>   and Pieter

and while I know
Robert would prefer
me to be one hundred percent
                  his

he knows better
than to ask
for impossibilities

because he knows
how I am, knows
who I am, knows
that only if I'm free
to choose

will I choose
to come
back.

The truth is

that spending some time apart
            will make both our hearts
                        fonder
            of each other
and I know this for a fact
            once I'm in Italy with Georg
                  and all I can talk about is how

he should join the International Brigades
now forming in Spain
to fight
for the republican cause
to fight
against fascism
because even in Italy
my thoughts keep returning
to Spain
my heart keeps returning
to *him*.

Especially when

the news out of Madrid
keeps filling
the papers
with headlines like

52 KILLED, 150 WOUNDED IN MADRID
AS 3 BOMBERS RAID ATOCHA STATION

and

HITLER CONFERS WITH MILITARY AIDES
ON SPAIN

painting a terrifying picture
of fascist General Franco

now in charge of the insurgent
troops
aided by German planes from
Hitler's Condor Legion
spreading over Spain

pummeling
the still-republican-held capital with
bombs
shells
bullets

making me desperate
to dive
back in.

TELEGRAM:
TO GERDA TARO, NAPLES

Still in Madrid, still alive STOP First time

close to combat truly terrifying STOP Meet

me in Paris

—Capa

MOTIVATION

I return from Italy to Paris where
I see Robert's triumphant work
      a photo of a shell-shocked woman
      surrounded by bombed-out rubble
with his name
           Capa
plastered
      right there on the front page
         of *Regards*

the magazine that gave
him the Madrid assignment

making my chest fill with pride
(and maybe a tiny bit of envy).

      Robert and his incredible work
        sticking close
      to the ideals we share

         that the republic
          and its people

          matter.

REUNION

In our downtime in Paris
Robert and I head

for Café du Dôme
where we swap

       stories
       kisses
       ideas

and conflicted feelings aside
over what I've missed
       in Spain

I'm excited to be planning
our next trip
            together

as soon
       as we can possibly
go.

WAITING

We pitch ourselves
to several magazines
                    hoping
for a joint assignment

but things move
            slowly
in December and
we must bide our time
the rest of the month

while being bombarded
with terrible headlines like

> FASTER PLANES RAINING
>
> DEATH OVER MADRID

waiting for our chance
to get back
to work.

Liebe Gerda

We're doing well enough here
though we all worry about you.
Please be careful if you go
back to Spain.

Once again, a scribbled note
from Oskar at the bottom

So proud (and a little envious)
of you, off fighting fascists.

Give one of them
a good punch from me.

MURCIA, SPAIN
JANUARY 1937

SOLO

Robert's still getting his papers in order
       so I head off for Spain first
without an assignment

but with
the two best gifts
I could have ever asked for:

Robert's own lightweight Leica
(now mine!)

a camera that once spent
as much time in the pawnshop
as in his hands

and

a rubber stamp
to mark my prints
no longer only Photo Capa

but instead

the glorious
Reportage Capa & Taro

and I've never
loved him

more.

ON THE COAST

I head to
      Valencia
on the Mediterranean

where I immerse
myself once more in
      the cause
      the news
meet up with friends
most of whom
are passing through with the
International Brigades

where I take pictures
retraining my hands and
my eyes to handle
the Leica

where I bide my time
preparing myself
to show the glory
and the truth
of this fight.

While waiting

I realize
that even in this
           hotbed
of a country at war
with itself

I feel safer here
than in my own homeland

safer than I do across its border
in my adopted one

because I realize that
                    here
no one scrutinizes
my name
my face
           wondering
if I'm Jewish

           at least partially because
           my natural looks blend in more here

but also because
the people of Spain have bigger

problems to worry about
             than me

and the freedom I feel
as one of them
rather than
             other
is a breath
          of sea-salt freshness
                 I didn't know
                 I needed.

ALMERÍA, SPAIN
FEBRUARY 1937
SANCTUARY

After a quick trip to Paris
I return to Spain with Robert

where we capture the scene
in Almería

          thousands of refugees
          shell-shocked from their flight

             from Málaga, where

an immense attack

by insurgent nationalist troops
aided by fascist Italian forces

has been underway for
the past few days

and is already almost
                    over

but

instead of word of
a great defense and stunning win

again
we hear of

broken, battered militia
hobbling away from their posts

accompanied by this flood
of women, children, everyone

        desperate
to escape fascist firing squads

descending
on the city.

JUXTAPOSITION

Just like I didn't think
    I'd hear
        the word *assassinate*
           about a poet
I didn't think
    I'd ever hear
        the words
           firing squad
                in the same sentence
           as *women* and *children*
but the world I once knew
    has clearly
been abandoned.

HUMAN FLOOD

With only one road
leading the way
northeast out
of Málaga

away from
insurgent

nationalist
forces

along a
rocky
curvy
coastline

streams of refugees
choke
the passage
desperate

to reach Almería
and the
relative
safety

where
we
await
them.

SNAPSHOT

Not only have these people left behind
    homes
        belongings
            lives
some have also left behind
    family
        friends
    whole entire hearts
but above all else
        when I focus, click, capture the moment
    what my viewfinder shows
        common to all these faces
young or old
    is that they've all
        left behind
    hope.

I can't help thinking

of my own family
    leaving their home
   everything they've known
       behind

because
for a family fleeing
the only thing
that truly matters
is their survival.

DESTINATION

After documenting
the plight of these refugees
highlighting
individual faces among the
tens of thousands fleeing

Robert and I move on
hearts heavy
leaving this tragedy
behind

head back toward
the center of
this country

the one
and only
Madrid.

MADRID, SPAIN
DINNER

When we reach
Madrid

we find a proud
            stubborn
city

its perimeter fortified
with troops and sandbags

with signs hanging
from balconies
bigger ones across streets

declaring

        ¡NO PASARÁN!

                (They shall not pass)

and we can only pray
it's true.

WARM WELCOME

As usual
most of the journalists
are staying at the Hotel Florida

but everyone gathers
in the basement
of the Hotel Gran Vía for
        dinner
        drinks
        discussion.

When we enter
they pounce
        asking Robert how he got
        such good photographs
        in Madrid

and after a moment
of silence and anticipation
his spontaneous response
is an instant classic.

If your pictures aren't good enough
you're not close enough.

The room erupts
in conversation and laughter
once more

and we hug and kiss
old friends
smile and greet
new ones
including a young and
wide-eyed Ted Allan
      fresh off the boat
      from Canada

and I'm thrilled to see
      poet Rafael Alberti
      his poetess wife, María León
who not only welcome
us to the city
but invite us to stay
at the Alianza
      also known as the
      Alianza de Intelectuales Antifascistas

because

although we're not exactly intelectuales
we're most decidedly antifascistas

so it sounds like
a suitable home
for us.

The Alianza

is located in an old palace
near the Paseo de Recoletos
with the Cibeles Fountain of
the goddess in her lion-drawn chariot

> which I capture in my viewfinder
> *click, whirr*
> as the statue is boarded up
> for protection from fascist bombs.

The Alianza is a residence filled
with authors
including Rafael and María
but also
Pablo Neruda
John Dos Passos
whose stimulating conversation
makes us feel at home right away

though María says
it's my smile and laughter
that puts everyone else

at ease.

She sets us up
in a two-room suite
with our very own bathroom
and while there's no such thing
as luxury during wartime
simply being here is
          the height of luxury
and we thrill in the luck
of experiencing it

as our sorrow fades away
                    replaced
with determination.

MONTH TO MONTH

This newfound feeling of luxury
is compounded
by success

          confidence!

when I fill out my paperwork
as a photographer
with the city of Madrid

noting *Ce soir*

        a new communist magazine
            in Paris

as my employer

                a magazine that calls
                Robert back to France
                on salary as well.

Not only do I have
        this fine place to stay
            now by myself

but

        this monthly salary
            all my own

María and the rest of the crowd
welcoming me back
after long days

        and I've never felt so lucky
           in my life.

SO MUCH HEART

María is by far
the kindest soul I've met
among many kind souls
        in Spain.

                Her tears when sharing that
                Federico García Lorca
                was not only a great poet
                        but a true friend.

                Her determination when sharing
                how she organized the evacuation
                of great works of Spanish art
                from El Escorial, Toledo, the Prado.

I can't help
wanting to change the world
        for the better
when around her

                the big sister
                I never had.

THE NIGHTLY SIEGE

The bombings
of Madrid have been bad
for months

      but

the nightly raids now
pummeling the city

          hum whistle boom blast

on repeat all through the night
drive the madrileños
                   underground
sending entire families
to basements
to metro stations

        anywhere

there's a chance
to survive.

In the basement at the Alianza

we
wait
heartbeats
thundering
wondering
if
one
of
these
breaths
will
be
our
last.

By day

I emerge from the Alianza
        pick my way west toward
                the university
            overwhelmed
by the destruction
        facades shorn clear away
                exposing buildings

like interiors of dollhouses
by the broken expressions
                    of those
        who've lost
                everything
by the smells
                of gunpowder
        dust and debris
                still-burning fires
and yet
        the republic

                        survives.

TO THE FRONT

Leaving bombed-out
Madrid behind

I prepare myself to visit
the front in Guadalajara
            northeast of the city

making sure
my camera and film
are in order but also

slipping into heels
applying a coat of lipstick
transforming myself

into a flag
to animate
the troops

before catching a ride with
a group of journalists
into battle

where generals and privates alike
crowd around me and my smile
                    buoyant

even more ready
than before
to take a stand.

ON REPEAT

I shoot
photos of bridges
compose
majestic views of soldiers

visit Guadalajara
day after day

and when masses of
Italian troops arrive
on the other side to aid
the fascist nationalists

I steel myself
for another defeat

but still head out
into the gray, wet, icy day
prepared to capture
       the action.

ATTACK

German pilots
have been aiding
the nationalist side and
attacking republican
       cities
         strongholds
         soldiers
for months now

so the drone of
approaching aircraft
through thick clouds
and a steady downpour
makes everyone

     slide

for safety

even when word
shoots down the line that
the planes attacking
this time aren't theirs

          but ours

a siege of unrelenting
bombs and bullets
turns the battlefield before us
into a muddy

     bloody

        mess.

SURPRISE

When it's all over
our side emerges

       virtually unscathed

and we cautiously step
around the now-quiet battlefield

where
       objects litter the ground.

As we creep closer
they come into focus
not objects at all but

       motionless bodies

along with
       broken pieces of flesh

             a head here
             a hand there

former people
       now in pieces.

My hand

flies to my face
   tries to block out
the metallic stench of

    blood
    flesh
    bodies

  baked in gunpowder
so strong and heavy
  I can't hold back
   the bile rising in my throat.

SNAPSHOT

After emptying
my stomach
I force myself to face
the bloodied bodies

  but the only pictures I take
   are with my eyes
 snap, snap, snap.

Heart heavy
I capture the carnage
return to the Alianza

unable
      unwilling
to forget.

María takes one look

at my shell-shocked face
      wraps her arms around me
            pulls me off to privacy
where I lay my head on her lap
      let loose a torrent of tears
            for those dead Italian boys
                  even if they were fighting for the
                  opposing side
until her calm sense of purpose manages to
      energize me
            to get back to work
                once more.

VALENCIA, SPAIN
A FRESH START

After Guadalajara
I regroup
reflect

pack my things and
head for Valencia

where the republican army
is growing, training, becoming
                    more disciplined
with help from
the Soviet Union

and I *snap, snap, snap*
photos of them
mobilizing in the Plaza de Toros.

Our militiamen look
like soldiers now

            marching in neat lines
                        wearing matching uniforms
                holding matching weapons

making it look
like we have a
fighting chance

but I can't help wondering
how much
this help from Russia
is going to

change us.

BUSINESS AND PLEASURE

Finished film rolls in hand
I return to Paris
to Robert

and it's good to see him
and we rush at each other
all kisses and news and
taking each other in

and afterward

we talk business
while we develop

roll after roll

       pride bursting
       across Robert's face
       when he sees
       what I've captured

and I'm ready
to get these latest
photos plastered
       everywhere
under my own name

and no sooner said
than Robert agrees
I should no longer submit
under Photo Capa or even
Reportage Capa & Taro

but

       Photo Taro

and I kiss him
all over again

       so pleased
              he's on my side.

UNEXPECTED

I'm flying so high
          soaring
      unaware

that I barely notice
Robert's asking me
a question.

                            Veux-tu m'épouser?

Words so simple
they stop my breath
in my throat

      his smile so earnest
         his eyes filled with love

and my heart swells
almost tempting
me to say *yes*

but I can't get married
      at least not right now

and I slowly shake
my head.

      It's not the right time.
      Not with so much wrong
            with this world.

And he understands, wraps
his arms around me, holds
the idea that maybe
      just maybe
our work can help
make this world
         change.

Liebe Familie

I'm back in Paris
but only momentarily

because each day
I spend in Spain

draws me to return
    to resist

those trying
to take it away

from its
people.

EXTREMES

BACK TO SPAIN

After a few more days in Paris
we arrive in Madrid
sweep into

       the Hotel Gran Vía's
       basement dining room

find the gang's all there
including a face already
familiar to many

          surrounded by all
     but new to me.

He lords over the room
puffing up his barrel of a chest
straightening his mustache
pushing up his glasses before
picking up his drink

      when he spots me
         and like most men

gives me the typical

head-to-toe sweep
  a glint in his eye
as I hover at the doorway
Robert at my elbow.

John Dos Passos calls
us over, introduces
us to the great
  Ernest Hemingway
who certainly seems to think
he's a gift to us all but
whose jaw clenches
when he discovers

I'm not someone's

    side dish

but instead
my very own
centerpiece.

THE SPANISH EARTH

Robert and Hemingway
hit it right off
blathering away

about Hem's plans to shoot
a documentary here
         in Spain

while I chat with Dos Passos
         who likewise seems less
         than enchanted with Hem

and when another woman enters
                  heads turn
just as they did for me
but instead of fixing my gaze
on her long blond bob
or her longer legs
for more than a moment

I turn, take in
these men around
the room ogling
her like an object

making me realize how
pathetic men can be

making me roll
my eyes before offering
the poor woman
a smile
         of solidarity.

INTRODUCTIONS

Not long after
Hem introduces
the leggy blonde
    Martha Gellhorn
    not just a beauty
    but a fellow journalist

Ted Allan arrives
eager as ever
and when I welcome
him with a rousing
    Hello, kid!

Robert and Dos grin
Martha raises an eyebrow
Hem rolls his eyes

    either annoyed
    that I have my own fans

        or annoyed
        that I'll never be his.

DAY IN, DAY OUT

The one thing
we all agree on
is that this republic
is worth fighting for

and when Hem invites Robert
      (and grudgingly, me)
to come along for
a day of filming

we follow
      me taking photos
        Robert trying out the filmmaker's
            Eyemo camera

capturing villagers
outside the city
working on farms to feed
the besieged city

and even in
their exhausted faces
we see belief
in our cause.

CELEBRATION

Before heading back to Paris
with our latest photos
Robert arranges
a small dinner party
at Casa Botín
near the Plaza Mayor

      with a paella
             unheard of in these
             times of scarcity

and when we raise
our glasses to toast
the farmers who work this land

       ¡Salud!

those reporting on it for the world

       ¡Salud!

those fighting for it
with their bodies, hearts, blood

¡Salud!

we revel in the conviction
that we'll continue
to champion this cause

with every last
          breath
in our bodies.

OUR LAST NIGHT

Bombers strike again
          hitting the heart of the city
aiming for anything
          they set their sights on

the Telefónica
Hotel Florida
other buildings on
Gran Vía

and once more I wonder
          how it is
that we're still here.

BACK IN PARIS

Robert and I indulge in
simple pleasures

quiet nights
      free of bomb blasts

            hot baths and
            a warm bed

an overabundance
of riches

      flaky croissants
            fresh flowers

and while it's a wonderful
escape being here

I'll never rest
until Spain is free.

Liebe Gerda

Although things remain
well enough here
we've again taken up
investigating our options

for the next stop
on our journey
because whether it be to
England, Palestine, or America

we know
the four of us
can't stay here
forever.

SUCCESS

After making our way through our
correspondence at the Hôtel de Blois
Robert and I catch up on the periodicals
that have piled up in our absence

plastered with

our photos
our names

and even if my first solo credit
misspells TARO as WARO

the next one

gets
it
right.

I can't help basking

in our success
for a moment

because

I know very well
that these publications
accept only dozens
of photographs

from thousands submitted

and sitting here
taking in our published work

is worth
                 so much to me.

HEADLINES

Once we're all caught up
we join Chim and Ruth
at a table at Café du Dôme, where
their identical grim expressions
                 greet us.

Chim wordlessly passes us
the *New York Herald Tribune*
its headline making us slump
in our seats

    AIR BOMBERS

    WIPE OUT FOUR

    BASQUE TOWNS

and then Ruth
adds to that
a copy of *Ce soir*
with even more details

IN THE RUINS OF GUERNICA

SPECIAL CORRESPONDENT

VISITS SURVIVORS

GERMAN PLANES
DROPPED THOUSANDS OF BOMBS
ON THE HISTORIC BASQUE TOWN

this news falling
on us like
whistling chunks
        of metal.

AFTERMATH

In the following days
we learn more

        about Guernica

attacked
        bombed
                razed
                to the ground

a brazen act aimed
not at soldiers
but civilians

        blown up

                        gunned down
             incinerated

so many
             innocent
                           lives

             stolen.

MEMORY

I squeeze my eyes shut
remember that day
in Guadalajara

             with the body parts
                        strewn about
             of those Italian boys
                               dead
                        at the front

how the sight of them
             blasted
a hole
through my heart

and even when I open

my eyes

my mind has only room for death

except this time it's
                women
                children
innocent civilians

ripped to
                        shreds
                by fascist
                                machines.

SHOCK

Every new detail that
emerges from Guernica
                thrusts me

                        beyond
rage at this injustice

                beyond
                        anguish at this suffering

especially the news that

the raid was carried out by
the German Condor Legion

my own countrymen
pummeling
        the land
        the people
I love

and now more than ever
I'm determined to
                make the world see

the human price
        of this struggle.

Liebe Familie

I'm sure you've heard
about the bombing of Guernica.

    (Yes, I'm safe.)
    (No, I wasn't there.)

But once again I'm relieved
you've escaped a land
that thinks nothing
of burning civilians

to
the
ground.

SNAPSHOT

It's a beautiful spring day
            in Paris
and Robert and I head for
the Place de la République
for the traditional parade
            ready
to catch the collective
energy of the crowds

        but first he captures
                    me
            snap, snap
        selecting a bunch of
        flowers as a sign of
                life

        so I do the same
        freezing the moment by
        stepping toward

him for a
bisou, bisou

and when we arrive
the crowd is already
        swelling

many of them carrying banners
            denouncing
the Guernica bombing
        calling attention to
                the carnage

and even on such a beautiful day
it's impossible
to forget.

VALENCIA, SPAIN
MAKING A DIFFERENCE

Robert is just as convinced
as I am that we need
to return
to Spain

        to document
        this destruction

and while he gets to work
          securing
the necessary paperwork

     (so much paperwork
          for a stateless person)

to travel to the Basque Country

     where fascist planes continue
     to carry out air raids
          on cities full
          of civilians

I head
to Valencia
on assignment

and we might be
          separate
in body

but we're
          together
in spirit.

TELEGRAM:
TO GERDA TARO, VALENCIA

Bilbao under siege STOP Much destruction STOP

Proud people with eyes to the sky STOP This

must end soon

—Capa

STRONGHOLD

In Valencia

        now the seat of the republican
            government

the streets stream with refugees
who've escaped
      horrors elsewhere

           horrors you can see
           burned in their eyes.

I aim to capture
a respite

from battle
from destruction

      a return to triumphant possibility

but that evening
at dusk

      the drone of fascist bombers
        fills the air.

AIR RAID

I tumble outside
       camera in hand
keeping at the doorway
for cover
where I spy through
my viewfinder
       the sky
       these narrow streets
       those fleeing
           with fear
           in their eyes

but it's already too dark
       to capture anything
           but night.

My heart hammers
as bombs strike targets
around the corner
down the block
sending stone and glass
and people

across the cobblestones
no longer sandy or gray

but black

              jagged

      red.

Afterward

the silence deafens
as I pick my way across
damaged streets
              homes
        lives

the wails
of a woman hunched
over a small body
        in the street

                 a mother

           her child

slicing into
my heart

sending tears
streaming down
my cheeks

        unbidden.

MORNING

I wake with the sun
      poke my head out
          the window
listen
      bits of building still crumbling
         people still sobbing
            my heart!
My bed pulls at me
      comforting as a mother's arms
but I remember my duty
      grab my camera, my film
and steel myself
      for the day ahead.

SNAPSHOT

I head for the one place
I know will bear
stark witness
to these events, and when

I arrive at the city morgue
I bypass the crowd

gathered at the gate
expressions grim

show my press pass
but before I march inside
with my Leica
I turn and

face this crowd waiting
for word about their
loved ones trapped
in the worst place of all

focus on their faces
and *click, click, click*
capture their dread
and hope on film.

Inside

bodies flop
        lifeless
on tables
                stretchers
and in the next room
        over the checkered floor
blood
        splattered from wounds

on clothing
                dried on corpses
        in clumps
bears testament
                to the cost of
        calculated killing
so as much as it hurts
my heart
        I must share this
                with the world.

ONE MORE STOP

After my visit to
the dead

I'm craving
signs of life

so I head upstairs
to the hospital

where I visit with
patients who survived

the bombing
reminding me

this republic
can withstand

anything.

TELEGRAM:
TO ROBERT CAPA, PARIS

Sending journalist with bombardment photos STOP

Print on high-contrast Kodak paper STOP Also

sending Córdoba front photos STOP Bring

floodlights and reflectors for movie camera STOP

Bring coffee and chocolate también

—Taro

THE OPPOSITE OF DESTRUCTION

I wind my way to Madrid
ring the bell at the Alianza
                    (home)

slip inside and rejoice
in María's
warm hugs

and when I tell her I still
need to see, need to share
                    hope

she mentions a nearby
orphanage freshly bursting
with new residents

and I grab my camera
load up a roll of film
let my feet lead me there.

SURVIVORS

My press pass once again
opens doors
and the sisters give me
full access to
children

      their skinny limbs and
            dark, immense eyes
      breaking my heart

but while they don't
smile for the camera

           and I wouldn't want them to

the fact that
they are here at all
is a victory

     proof

           that the Spain their parents fought for
                will flourish.

REUNION

Robert arrives
at the end of the month

and we grasp each other close
affirming our aliveness

before getting
down to business.

He's brought
everything I asked for

and we can't talk fast enough
as we share

everything we've seen
these past weeks

the terror of the bombings
the toll on individuals

and we decide
what we need to do

is to get
right back out there.

The Navacerrada Pass

is beautiful
     secretive
   deadly

with our troops from the
     International Brigades dug into
   the wooded hills

     where we move among
        their camouflaged dugouts
     taking photos
   in this magic-hour light

       their expressions
    serious for the camera

       but

      smiley, relaxed
    once we put the cameras away.

We eat together

chicken and wine at
            a makeshift table
    with General Walter and his men

all of us silently wondering
        as they prepare to take
            the offensive
if the meal will be someone's last.

BATTLE

It begins
all at once
our tanks grinding
                forward
men following
rifles at the ready

        and we stay close

but

insurgent troops
open fire too
their planes fill
the sky

and we stay low

in the chaos
the confusion
that mounts all around us
until we're not sure
which direction is
                    forward
            and which is
back
as bullets graze
trees
helmets
even my camera

        and we stay alive.

DOWNWARD SPIRAL

We follow the action
for the full day, then
return to Madrid

where we soon learn
of more terrible news

BILBAO FALLS

and it's hard not to get
discouraged

as we arrange to visit
the Córdoba front
one more time.

CELEBRITIES

International troops
American, Canadian, French
even German
welcome us to their camp with
giant smiles
enthusiasm
respect

and even though I no longer wear
heels and lipstick but
everyday alpargatas and coveralls

a circle forms
around me

like I'm a film star

A lady reporter!
And she speaks German!

Wine and whiskey flow
as they agree to let Robert film
a short motion picture
while I follow with the Leica

and as petite
and feminine
as I am
in such a
manly world

I think these soldiers
would follow me
                    anywhere

little me
            their glorious flag.

GREAT LITERARY MINDS

After our time in the field
Robert and I take a respite

covering a writers' conference
in Valencia

led by friends from the Alianza
including María

and when the conference
returns to Madrid

I go
with it
with them

while Robert
returns to Paris
telling Ted Allan

I leave Gerda
in your charge, Teddie.
Take good care of her.

But I simply roll
my eyes at
the chivalry because

        I can take care of

                myself.

MADRID, SPAIN
Back in Madrid

means back to normal
    with activity all day
        (photographing the conference)
    artillery blasts all night
        around the Alianza

and though I love
these authors and
how they use their words
to fight this fight

an itch, urge, want
drives me
to get back out there
to get to the action

    to get that shot

that makes a difference

especially
that night at dinner
with all the journalists
                    twitchy
for news

when the doors burst open
and three republican soldiers march in
waving a battle-worn
nationalist flag
over their heads
in victory.

SNAPSHOT

My shutter clicks
            once, twice
capturing these soldiers
                    who've
captured this flag

and I rewind the roll
send it off to Paris
with a request for
                permission

from *Ce soir*
        to let me stop
covering this conference

so I can record
what's going on
at the front in Brunete
        (now under republican control)
           instead.

BRUNETE

I'm prepared to go
to the front alone
with my camera

but every day I set off
another journalist asks
to tag along

and I'm happy to share
the ride, the experience
of observing

the scope of preparations
for a battle like nothing
I've ever seen

with seventy thousand troops
guns, tanks, planes
amassed and ready

General Walter
discussing strategy
with other officers

but before more
fighting gets underway
I stop, breathe, take in

this village formerly held
by nationalists
handed back to us like

a baby
swaddled
in a tattered blanket.

THE OFFENSIVE

When the push gets
underway
battle lines are
blurred

a cacophony of chaos
                reigns
as casualties mount

while I try my best
to bear witness
to what feels like
        a historic

beginning
of the
end.

SINKING IN

That night I dine
at the Alianza, wanting
the comfort of
        home
        friends
an affirmation of
                life
and we sit silently slurping
our lentils in weak broth.

Across from me
        Pablo Neruda

whose new booklet of poetry
España en el corazón
(*Spain in the Heart*)
travels to the front
in republican pockets
must be struggling to contain
a multitude of feelings
so I swallow
dare to express my own anxieties.

I can't help thinking
of all the fine people we know
who've been killed
in this war.
It's almost absurd
how unfair it is
to still be
alive.

The silence over the table
hangs heavier now
as my words sink in

even to me.

TELEGRAM:
TO GERDA TARO, MADRID

Still looking for new assignments STOP If there's

a lull in the action come to Paris STOP Bastille

Day and kisses await

—Capa

PARIS, FRANCE
CELEBRATION

I take Robert up
on his invitation and

the streets of Paris
bustle with life

especially on July 14
the national celebration

      Bastille Day.

We head to Montmartre
eat, drink, dance with friends

almost forgetting
all the suffering

in other parts
of the world

if only for
one day.

Liebe Gerda

We hope
you're staying safe
while in Spain
(and enjoying a respite in Paris).

Good news to share
from the four of us:

we've applied
for clearance
to emigrate
to Palestine

and hope to
be able to
write you from there
soon.

I grasp
the letter
to my chest

      gasp my relief.

WORLD'S FAIR

With only one more day
before I return to Madrid

Robert and I decide to head
to the International Exposition

which has been running
since late spring here in Paris

and although the Spanish Pavilion
opened only recently

everything we hear about
the artists' work

tells us what we're going to see
will impress us.

FAIRGROUNDS

When we arrive, we can't ignore
the massive monuments of
the showpieces on the banks of

the Seine

Germany's on one side
        an immense tower
        topped with an eagle

                How can this be
                my former homeland?

Russia's on the other
        shorter but nonetheless massive
        topped with a man and woman
                holding a hammer and sickle

and we roll our eyes at how
they try to outdo each other.

They both loom large
over tiny Spain
which we finally find
beyond that

attracting
        loads
of attention.

MASTERPIECES

The Spanish Pavilion itself is
    small
    utilitarian
    modern

        with a photomural
        hung right at the entrance

and once inside
we pass wordlessly by
amazing works
of art

a mural painted by Joan Miró

     a mercury fountain by Alexander Calder
        honoring the workers we witnessed
           in the mines at Almadén

and the greatest masterpiece
    of them all

a piece entitled
    Guernica

by Pablo Picasso
that was painted
over the past weeks in his
studio right here in Paris

but that
        amazingly
accurately captures
the brutality
        of this war
in black and white and gray

                people screaming
                bodies in pieces
                flames, suffering, horror

the human cost
        of lives lost
        immorality gained.

CONFLICTED

As deeply as I'm
invested in this conflict

I'm
  torn

between my desire to
document the continued fight

and my desperation
    to avoid

witnessing the fall
of this republic

   if it should come
      to that in the end.

PLANS

Robert understands
why I waver

and as I pack
my bag for
my return to Madrid

he offers an alternative.

Things are heating up
in China.

He points to the latest
New York Herald Tribune
with the headline

BATTLES RAGE

CHINA, JAPAN

FORESEE WAR

I'm going to push harder to get
an assignment to go there next.
You'll come along, won't you?

Once again
his deep eyes so full
of love.

I pause for a moment
taking him in
considering
this way out
before replying

Why not?

and like that
an inkling of a spark of

a new, different adventure
with my copain
lights a fire

     in my heart
          once more.

I buckle my bag closed
send a smile
across the room.

    I'll be back
    in ten days

and he rushes
toward me, crushing
me close in his arms
as if he might never
see me
    again.

MADRID, SPAIN
Upon my return

to Madrid, I learn
that things are heating
up again at Brunete
with headlines like

FRANCO BATTERS MADRID ROAD
7,000 CASUALTIES

which make me
              anxious
to get back out there
to share with the world
what's happening

especially now
that I know
these might be my

last
days
here

and I don't waste
any time preparing
myself and my cameras

for my last chance
to capture
what I hope
will be an important
victory.

BACK TO BRUNETE

It's even harder these days
to secure an authorized car
to get out to the front

with the censor
denying
all journalists access.

I leave her
a bouquet of flowers
because she's only doing her job

and instead, I find
other means
to get there.

Once we reach the searing-hot fields
we rush for carved trenches
that bake bodies

while
deadly noises
assault our ears

whistle
boom
blast.

Sometimes our side takes
the offensive
running toward the fascist line

while sometimes
we huddle in place
pummeled by explosions

wondering
if this day
will be our last.

TELEGRAM:
TO GERDA TARO, MADRID

We have assignment with Life magazine STOP When

you arrive we're off to China STOP Champagne

chilling

—Capa

ONE MORE DAY

That night I tell Ted and the others
at the Alianza about the assignment

thrilled about the
new adventure in China

and they're all just as
happy for me

even Ted
smiling like the rest

     despite evident envy
          over my adventuring

          coupled with overt jealousy
               over what I have with Robert

but I kiss him on the cheek
punch him in the shoulder

ask him if he wants
to go to the front tomorrow

because before I pack
my bag, I still have

one last chance
to get the best shots

and since he's the one
                    here

he's the one
who can come along

        for the ride.

PERMISSION DENIED

The next morning
when Ted and I get to the front
we find General Walter
          normally so happy to see me
pointing his finger away
              yelling

Not today!
You must go immediately!
It's going to be hell
any minute now.

Ted agrees, wants to
get out of here
but I convince him
to sneak around the situation
find another way in.

Franco's troops have recaptured
                    Brunete
bitter clashes erupt
with gunshots exchanged
            in the streets
            in the fields
            everywhere

and we live a day filled
with the rush of

            adrenaline
shock
            danger.

SNAPSHOT

My shutter *click*, *clicks*
            capturing
blurry soldiers on the move

tanks, planes, artillery
a truck on fire

action, action, action

in the most
terrifying yet exhilarating
day of my life

and although Ted tries again
          and again
to get me to leave

                             Come on, Gerda.
                             It's not safe.

I'm not done yet
not until I get

one
last
shot.

At the end of the day

I finish my last
roll of film
we follow the troops

now in retreat
trying to hitch a ride
out of here.

We make it to the
road we came in on
spot a big black car

General Walter's!

He's not inside
and instead it's
filled with wounded
but still it's

our only chance out

so I step
on the running board
on one side
while Ted hangs on
to the other

and we're ready
to ride.

UNFINISHED BUSINESS

We're barely underway
when German planes approach
      this time flying low.

Our driver guns it
            but

one of our own tanks comes out of nowhere
        clearly doesn't see us
slams into the car

with a
horrifying
metallic
creak

and I'm flying
through the air, flying
toward this hard
Spanish earth, flying
into the tank, its treads
suddenly on top
of my tiny body

ripping

me to shreds.

I scream

from the pain
from the horror
because when the tank
moves off me seconds later

my terror has only begun
as I look down, take in

my insides splayed
outside

my life
slipping

through fingers
trying to hold
it all in.

EMERGENCY

It seems like forever
and no time at all

Ted's voice calling
out for me

from somewhere as far
away as the sun

someone radioing
for an ambulance

which unbelievably arrives
with medics whose faces

seal in the hopelessness
of my fate as they load

me on a stretcher
get me inside.

A REQUEST

Once in the hospital
they prepare
me for surgery
        (without anesthesia).
I grasp the nurse's arm
gasp out the words

        Please. My cameras.

Her lips press together
in silent recognition
of the seriousness
of the situation

of the seriousness
of this

        most likely
my last wish.

She meets my gaze
                steady
        nods

allowing me to close my eyes
and rest easy.

SNAPSHOT

I hold
    everyone I love
        in my heart

           my parents
           Oskar, Karl
      Meta, Pieter, Ruth, Georg
        María, Ted
        Robert

           floating
        floating
eyes closed

    but

photographs flash
through the viewfinder
in my mind

      aperture closing now

signs

that even once I'm gone

a part of me

might

remain.

DRAMATIS PERSONAE

Rafael Alberti and María León were both poets. A married couple on the republican side, they supported the arts—and artists—at the Alianza de Intelectuales Antifascistas in Madrid. After the republican defeat in the Spanish Civil War, the couple fled to Paris and then Argentina, where they remained in exile before returning to Spain in 1977.

Ted Allan was a Canadian writer who covered the Spanish Civil War as a reporter with the International Brigades. He later wrote a semi-autobiographical novel about his experiences called *This Time a Better Earth*.

Ernestine (Terra) Boral and Moritz Pohoryles were Gerda's well-off aunt and uncle, who helped Gerda's family when they first moved to Stuttgart and as the children were growing up. They also left Germany for Petrovgrad, and were most likely murdered in 1941 or 1942 after the nazis entered and occupied Yugoslavia.

Gisela (Gittel) Boral and Heinrich (Hersch) Pohorylle were Gerda's parents. Originally from Galicia (in modern-day

Ukraine but previously part of Poland), they moved to Stuttgart before Gerda was born. After Gerda left Germany for Paris, they stayed in Leipzig until moving to Petrovgrad in the former Yugoslavia (in modern-day Serbia). Gisela died of an illness in 1937. Because it was unclear whether this was before or after Gerda's death, I decided not to mention it. Heinrich was most likely murdered in 1941 or 1942 after the nazis entered and occupied Yugoslavia.

Hans (Pieter) Bote was Gerda's fiancé, although he was quite a bit older than her. He remained friendly and supportive of Gerda even after they broke off their engagement. He was not Jewish, so after the Nuremberg Laws of 1935, their union would have been illegal.

Julia and Cornell Capa (originally Friedmann) were Robert's mother and brother. They traveled to Paris in 1936 and waited there for their visas to emigrate to New York, where they both adopted Robert's new last name as well.

Robert Capa (October 23, 1913–May 25, 1954) was born as Endre Ernő Friedmann (later André Friedmann) in Budapest, Hungary. He left his homeland after his arrest and release to study in Berlin, and then emigrated to Paris after the nazis came to power. Though he was linked to many women after Gerda's death, he never got over her. He is considered one of the greatest war photographers, and died stepping on a land mine on assignment in Vietnam in 1954.

Ruth Cerf was one of Gerda's best friends in Leipzig and Paris. She was Jewish. She left Paris in 1939 for Switzerland, where she survived the war. Biographer Irme Schaber was able to interview her.

Willi Chardack was a student and part of Gerda's circle in both Leipzig and Paris, where he was briefly a boyfriend. He emigrated to New York from Marseilles, France, and became a doctor.

Chim (November 20, 1911–November 10, 1956) was born as Dawid Szymin in Warsaw, Poland, and was later known as David Seymour. Chim studied in Leipzig and Paris, where he became a photographer. He covered the Spanish Civil War and other conflicts, and was killed in action in Egypt in 1956.

John Dos Passos was the American author of the successful USA trilogy, among other works. Owing to his socialist and pacifist views, he served as an ambulance driver in World War I and covered the Spanish Civil War. His experiences there led to disillusionment and eventually changed his political views.

Maria Eisner started Alliance Photo agency. A friend of Robert's from his Berlin days, she offered Gerda a job in Paris. When World War II began, she emigrated to New York, where years later she and five other photojournalists, including Robert and Chim, founded Magnum Photo.

Francisco Franco was a general in the Spanish army and one of the leaders of the coup that aimed to wrest control of Spain from the legitimate republican government. He took charge of the nationalist forces in 1936 and led them to victory in the Spanish Civil War in 1939. Spain then became a dictatorship under his control until his death in 1975.

Federico García Lorca was a poet and playwright of critically acclaimed works. He was also a gay man and a socialist who counted Rafael Alberti and María León as well as Salvador Dalí and many other creative people among his friends. He was murdered by the nationalist militia in August 1936.

Martha Gellhorn was an American war correspondent who covered conflicts including the Spanish Civil War and World War II. She also wrote novels and a memoir, but is often more known for her marriage to Hemingway than her own accomplishments.

Ernest Hemingway was an American author of many acclaimed works, including *For Whom the Bell Tolls*, a novel based on his experiences in the Spanish Civil War. He married four times; his third wife was journalist Martha Gellhorn. He won the Nobel Prize in Literature in 1954.

Georg Kuritzkes was a Jewish student who was active in Leipzig's left-leaning political scene before leaving to study in Italy. He was one of Gerda's boyfriends, and they remained close even after she met Robert Capa. She inspired him to join the International Brigades to fight in Spain. He survived the Spanish Civil War and World War II and became a doctor.

Pablo Neruda was a Chilean poet who served as the consul in Madrid, where he was close friends with Rafael Alberti and María León and their friends at the Alianza. His collection *España en el corazón* was a testament to his belief in the republican cause. He later served as consul in Mexico City and as a senator in Chile before going into exile for his communist political views. He won the Nobel Prize in Literature in 1971.

Oskar and Karl Pohorylle were Gerda's younger brothers. From what little is known of them, they were as left-wing as Gerda was, so it's unclear why they didn't leave Germany with or after her (although likely both to make things easier on Gerda— since they didn't speak French—and to stay with and help their parents). They were most likely murdered in 1941 or 1942 after the nazis entered and occupied Yugoslavia.

Meta Schwarz was Gerda's best friend in Stuttgart, who went with her to finishing school in Switzerland. She was not Jewish. She remained in Stuttgart, where she survived the war, and biographer Irme Schaber was able to interview her.

Fred and Liselotte (Lilo) Stein fled Germany in 1933 for Paris, where Fred began working as a photographer because he was unable to work there as a lawyer. They took in other émigrés, including Gerda Taro, at their flat. After World War II began, the couple eventually escaped Paris for Marseilles and traveled to New York on the same ship as Willi Chardack.

Gerda Taro (August 1, 1910–July 26, 1937) was born as Gerta Pohorylle in Stuttgart, Germany. To keep things simpler here, I used the Gerda spelling of her name throughout, but she and André Friedmann did come up with their working names together (Robert Capa and Gerda Taro) when living in Paris. She was the first known female photojournalist killed on the battlefield (in Brunete, Spain).

Lucien Vogel was a French editor and director of several publications, including *Vu*, a photo-heavy magazine that was the first to publish Robert's photos under his pseudonym. He also arranged the first trip that brought Gerda and the others to Spain.

General Walter was the nickname of Karol Świerczewski, a Polish and Soviet general who was one of the leaders of the International Brigades in many battles, including Brunete.

AUTHOR'S NOTE

INSPIRATION

Spain holds a place in my heart like no other. It's a beautiful country that still bears the scars of its violent civil war, which went on from 1936 to 1939. I've been interested in this period of the country's history since I first started visiting Spain in the early 2000s, but it was only when I came across Gerda Taro that I found a way to tell this more personal story about the conflict.

I first learned about Gerda when the 2018 Google Doodle honored her on her birthday. I've been an amateur black-and-white photographer myself since high school, and I knew who Robert Capa was, but I'd never heard of this impish-looking girl holding the camera in the Doodle. The more I learned about Gerda, the more I loved her: her profoundly anti-fascist views, her fierce dedication to sharing the right side of the story, her charm, her unrivaled confidence, and above all, her perfectly balanced combination of femininity and toughness. For all these reasons, Gerda grabbed hold of me as a YA protagonist, and I simply couldn't get enough of her.

FACT OR FICTION

The majority of the people I've represented here are based on real people: Gerda Taro (born Gerta Pohorylle), Robert Capa (born Endre, later André, Friedmann), and the bulk of Gerda's family and friends. A few liberties I took in naming characters are Meta's Onkel Friedrich—I couldn't track down his actual name—and Gerda and Meta's classmates at finishing school, whose names I couldn't determine either.

In trying my very best to stick to the facts as known, I am indebted to Gerda's biographers Irme Schaber and Jane Rogoyska for publishing such thorough works, which include many of the anecdotes I fictionalized here. Irme Schaber in particular was able to conduct interviews with individuals who knew Gerda well, including Meta Schwarz, Ruth Cerf, Georg Kuritzkes, and Willi Chardack.

However, this is a novel, not a biography, so I've taken the liberty of fictionalizing what goes beyond these basic facts, including Gerda's thoughts, feelings, interactions, and correspondence. She left behind no diary or letters, and because her entire family was murdered in the Holocaust, much of the interaction I show is imagined. One exception is the telegram Gerda sent Robert from Spain to Paris asking him to bring specific items, which is based on an actual telegram.

While fictionalizing these personal aspects of the story, I tried my best to paint an accurate picture of this incredibly charged time. To that end, I included newspaper headlines from various periodicals, including the *Vossische Zeitung* from Berlin; *Paris-soir*, *Regards*, *Ce soir*, and *Vu* from Paris; the European edition of the

New York Herald; *El Debate* and *ABC* from Madrid; and *ABC* from Seville in Spain. *ABC* continues to be published today as a relatively conservative paper, but during the civil war, the Seville edition was a nationalist paper and the Madrid edition a republican one. It's pretty incredible to see the different takes on some of the same events from these two papers.

As far as visuals from the era go, the best and most wonderful sources are the photographs themselves, above all those by Gerda and Robert. Most of these can be seen at the International Center of Photography (ICP), an organization founded by Robert's brother, Cornell. It operates a fantastic, searchable website where you can see Gerda's talent from anywhere in the world for yourself.

THE SPANISH CIVIL WAR

The Spanish Civil War was an incredibly complicated conflict, and the story I tell here covers only a slice of it—both in time, as this story covers only the first year of the three-year war, and in perspective, as Gerda's naturally biased view as someone fiercely connected to one side would have given her little if any insight into the opposite side's motivations or suffering.

The truth is that both sides committed terrible atrocities, starting in the first months of the war. The murder of poet Federico García Lorca by nationalist forces was a painful example of this to Gerda and those on the republican side. But republican forces were also guilty of committing atrocities, including murdering many members of the clergy and others suspected of aiding those who had launched the coup.

I didn't include much of Gerda's reaction to republican atrocities because it's quite likely she didn't know the details, as propaganda was deftly channeled. One exception to this was the deaths of the inexperienced Italian soldiers at Guadalajara. They died in battle—not as part of an atrocity campaign—but witnessing the aftermath of their destruction was certainly an eye-opening view for Gerda to the suffering of the opposing side.

After Gerda's death, other reprisals continued on both sides, with the biggest reprisals at the end of the war after the nationalist victory. Republicans fled the country to avoid concentration camps, and many who remained either wound up in these camps or were killed outright.

Francisco Franco led the cobbled-together country that remained after the war as a dictator, without free elections and without involving anyone who had been on the republican side, until his death in 1975. When the war ended in 1939, Franco's new government produced a document called *Dictamen de la comisión sobre ilegitimidad de poderes actuantes en 18 de julio de 1936*. This report attempted to justify the nationalist coup that launched the country into civil war by calling into question the election the Frente Popular won in February 1936.

LEGACY

With the 2007 discovery of the "Mexican Suitcase" collection of 4,500 Spanish Civil War negatives, Gerda Taro was finally fully recognized for her work as a photographer.

When World War II started back in 1939, Robert entrusted the negatives to his darkroom manager in Paris, requesting they be sent on to his destination in New York. The negatives didn't arrive. With the loss of this work went the bulk of Gerda's output, and she was forgotten—until the discovery of the "Mexican Suitcase."

The "suitcase"—which wasn't actually a suitcase, but a set of three boxes containing rolls of negatives—had been carried by the Mexican ambassador from France to Mexico City, where it sat in storage. Only years later did the ambassador's nephew realize the significance of the items. He delivered the boxes to the ICP, where the items were examined and archived—and where it was determined that about a third of the photographs were shot by Gerda. (Another third were shot by Chim, and another third by Robert.)

The first exhibition of the contents was held at the ICP in 2010, and a 2011 documentary called *The Mexican Suitcase* covers the mystery of the items' loss and recovery, along with the painful repercussions of the civil war that still run through Spain today. Now that Gerda's work as one of the most important photographers to document that conflict has finally been recognized, I hope this version of her story prompts even more people to discover the incredible person behind the camera.

ACKNOWLEDGMENTS

As I mentioned in the author's note, Spain holds a place in my heart like no other. My immense thanks to Bernardo for introducing me to this beautiful country, and to the entire Rechea family for welcoming an American twenty years ago whose first efforts to speak Spanish came out in German. Muchas gracias por todo, abuelita Marta; hermanos Cecilia, Agustín, María José, Charo y Taeksoo; tíos Cristina, Alfredo, Pilar, Rafa, Miguel, Pili, Carmen y Juan Manuel; y primos Pedro, Lolín, Cristina, Rafa, Gema, Jaime, David, Lucas y Tomás.

A huge thank-you as well to my incredible agent, Roseanne Wells (for everything!), and to everyone at Versify who touched this manuscript on its way to becoming a book, including Kwame Alexander, Margaret Raymo, Ciera Burch, Monica Perez, and most especially Liz Agyemang for shepherding Gerda's story through the editorial process. Thank you also to artist Mark Smith and designer David Curtis for the gorgeous cover; to production editor Erika West and copyeditors Valerie Shea and Jeffrey Evatt; and to John Sellers, Sammy Brown, and everyone else in sales, marketing, and publicity for all your efforts. Thanks also to my sensitivity readers and language experts for the most helpful feedback and corrections. I appreciate you so much!

As always, no book would have made it this far without critique partners and readers. A huge and special thanks to Monica Ropal, Michelle Mason, Marley Teter, Shari Green, Kerri Maher, and Carrie Callaghan for reading Gerda's full story and helping me make it better. Thank you to my critique group, the LitWits—Joan Paquette, Julie Phillipps, and Natalie Lorenzi—and my verse novel critique group—Rebecca Caprara, Rebekah Lowell, and Krista Surprenant—for reading many chunks and iterations along the way. Thank you to my fellow early risers at #5amWritersClub and my fellow history nerds at #HFChitChat and in the Historical Novel Society.

On the research side, I wouldn't have been able to write this book without a few important sources. I'm extremely grateful to the International Center of Photography (ICP) in New York for making Gerda Taro's photographs accessible online, and I am especially indebted to Cynthia Young's efforts in curating the materials discovered in the "Mexican Suitcase." Along with the photographs themselves, two excellent biographies of Gerda Taro were indispensable to me: I thank Irme Schaber and Jane Rogoyska for these incredibly thorough works and for answering my remaining questions. Thank you also to author Helena Janeczek, whose novel about Gerda Taro further piqued my interest and who likewise kindly answered some additional questions.

I'm also grateful for several fabulous historians in Spain. Thank you to Alan Warren, Alicia, and Ángel for taking me around the Brunete area; to Ernesto Viñas and Sven Tuytens for all your work on Brunete en la Memoria; and to Almudena Cros for your unrelenting help in Madrid.

As always, books only get written (and revised, and revised again) with the support from the author's circle of nonwriting people, and my inner circle includes my wonderful daughters, Mae, Lyra, and Violeta; my dad; my brother, Matt; my sister-in-law, Catherine; and my friend-for-more-years-than-I-can-count, Rosanne. Thank you all for being there for me.

Finally, thank *you*, reader, for stepping into the past on this journey through Gerda Taro's extraordinary life with me. I hope she captivates you as much as she did me, and I hope her passion will inspire you to fight for your beliefs with your entire heart.

SELECTED SOURCES

SOURCES IN ENGLISH

Aronson, Marc, and Marina Budhos. *Eyes of the World: Robert Capa, Gerda Taro, and the Invention of Modern Photojournalism.* New York: Henry Holt and Company, 2017.

Beevor, Antony. *The Battle for Spain: The Spanish Civil War 1936–1939.* New York: Penguin Books, 2006.

Capa, Robert. *Death in the Making.* Bologna: Damiani, 1938.

Frizot, Michel, and Cédric de Veigy. *Vu: The Story of a Magazine.* London: Thames & Hudson, 2009.

García Lorca, Federico. *Selected Poems.* New York: New Directions Books, 1955.

Hemingway, Ernest. *For Whom the Bell Tolls.* New York: Charles Scribner's Sons, 1940.

Horenstein, Henry. *Black and White Photography: A Basic Manual.* New York: Little, Brown and Company, 1983.

Janeczek, Helena. *The Girl with the Leica.* Translated by Ann Goldstein. New York: Europa Editions, 2019.

Kershaw, Alex. *Blood and Champagne: The Life and Times of Robert Capa*. New York: Macmillan, 2002.

Maspero, François. *Out of the Shadows: A Life of Gerda Taro*. London: Souvenir, 2008.

Neruda, Pablo. *Spain in our Hearts: España en el corazón*. Translated by Donald Walsh. New York: New Directions Books, 2005.

New York Herald (Paris), October 1933–July 1937.

Richarz, Monika, ed. *Jewish Life in Germany: Memoirs from Three Centuries*. Bloomington: Indiana University Press, 1991.

Rogoyska, Jane. *Gerda Taro: Inventing Robert Capa*. London: Jonathan Cape, 2013.

Vaill, Amanda. *Hotel Florida: Truth, Love, and Death in the Spanish Civil War*. New York: Farrar, Straus and Giroux, 2014.

Wallach, Kerry. *Passing Illusions: Jewish Visibility in Weimar Germany*. Ann Arbor: University of Michigan Press, 2017.

Whelan, Richard. *Robert Capa: A Biography*. New York: Knopf, 1985.

SOURCES IN OTHER LANGUAGES

ABC (Madrid), July 1936–July 1937.

ABC (Seville), July 1936–July 1937.

Ce soir (Paris), March–July 1937.

El Debate (Madrid), February–July 1936.

Guerra de la Vega, Ramón. *Madrid 1931–1939: II República y Guerra Civil*. Madrid: Street Art Collection, 2005.

León, María Teresa. *Memoria de la melancolía*. Seville: Editorial Renacimiento, 2020.

Mendelson, Jordana. *El pabellón español París, 1937*. Barcelona: Edicions de la Central, 2010.

Paris-soir (Paris), October 1933–July 1937.

Pérez-Reverte, Arturo. *La guerra civil contada a los jóvenes*. Barcelona: Penguin Random House Grupo Editorial, 2016.

Regards (Paris), October 1933–July 1937.

Schaber, Irme. *Gerta Taro: Fotoreporterin im spanischen Bürgerkrieg: Eine Biografie* [*Gerda Taro: Photojournalist in the Spanish Civil War: A Biography*]. Marburg, Germany: Jonas Verlag, 1994.

Vossische Zeitung (Berlin), May 1929–April 1933.

FILMS AND OTHER MEDIA

British Pathé. Spanish Civil War footage. www.britishpathe.com/workspaces/page/spanish-civil-war-1.

ICP Gerda Taro photographs. www.icp.org/browse/archive/constituents/gerda-taro?all/all/all/all/0.

ICP Mexican Suitcase photographs. www.icp.org/exhi=bitions/the-mexican-suitcase-traveling-exhibition; www.icp.org/browse/archive/collections/the-mexican-suitcase.

Interview with biographer Jane Rogoyska. jewishbookweek.com/event/jane-rogoyska-gerda-taro-and-photojournalism.

Ivens, Joris. The Spanish Earth. Contemporary Historians, Inc., 1937. www.youtube.com/watch?v=MT8q6VAyTi8.

Presentation by biographer Irme Schaber. www.youtube.com/watch?v=l0KDjo8T7wo.

Presentation by ICP curator Cynthia Young. www.youtube.com/watch?v=tNrjqkI3Jnc.

Radio interview with Robert Capa. www.youtube.com/watch?v=MYe4ynXnqug.

Ziff, Trisha. The Mexican Suitcase. 212 Berlin, 2011. tubitv.com/movies/169519/the-mexican-suitcase.

GLOSSARY

GERMAN
Anderssein: being other
blitzschnell: lightning fast
Familie: family
Hauptbahnhof: main train station
jawohl: absolutely
Königin-Charlotte-Realschule: Queen Charlotte Secondary
　　School
Liebe: dear
Onkel: uncle
Reich: empire
Reichstag: parliament
Tante: aunt
Tanzorchester: dance orchestra
Trauerbinde: armband worn in mourning
Umzug: parade
Zellerstraße: Zeller Street

FRENCH

à bientôt: see you

arrondissements: districts

au revoir: good-bye

bisou: kiss

bonjour: hello, good day

centime: penny

charmant: charming

le chef: the boss

copain: pal, boyfriend

escargot: snail

fausse: fake

flirter: flirt

Front Populaire: Popular Front

Gare de l'Est: east train station

Jardin du Luxembourg: Luxembourg Garden

Je t'adore: I adore you

Je t'aime: I love you

joie de vivre: joy of life

mais oui: that's right

Quartier Latin: Latin Quarter

parler: speak

sourire: smile

un, deux, trois: one, two, three

Veux-tu m'épouser?: Do you want to marry me?

vin de table: table wine

SPANISH

alcázar: fortress

Alianza de Intelectuales Antifascistas: Alliance of Anti-Fascist
Intellectuals

alpargatas: rope-soled canvas sandals

aventuras en España: adventures in Spain

barras de pan: loaves of bread

Frente Popular: Popular Front

madrileños: people from Madrid

No pasarán: They shall not pass

la pequeña rubia: the little blonde

Regresaremos, mi amor: We'll return, my love

salud: cheers

Semana Santa: Holy Week

señorita: miss

también: too